Hard Case

Fight Like A Girl, Part Three

Stratford Police Department

900 Longbrook Ave.

Stratford, Connecticut

June, 2008

"Okay, Moon Girl; Harpie and Pig Face here say you're good with ….. corn-puters," Clodagh said to Tanner Lee as she smiled at Carla.

"Watch it, ketchup head; you are on thin ice," Carla nodded.

"I don't get it; you keep telling us you speak Kansasian; why do you think we're making fun of you when we speak it?" Clodagh said. "It is to our benefit to be able to communicate with assholes, isn't it?"

"I speak Cocker Spaniel, too, but you do not hear me barking, do you?" Carla said.

"That makes no sense," Clodagh said as Tanner Lee watched the festivities.

"Fuck you," Carla grinned. "Right up your scrawny ass. Do that make sense?"

"In case you haven't noticed, I'm quite a bit bigger now, and in all the right places," Clodagh said. "Unlike you; you're sitting on your biggest asset, with the accent on ass."

"Can we stop the insults and do some work? I have to renew my subscription to UFO Monthly," Tanner Lee said. "Humans," she sighed. "Looking at you disgusting specimens make me ashamed to be one. Fortunately, I was raised by the Pleiadians, so I do not share your violent, perverted personality traits "

"Then go back to fuckin' Mars where you came from," Carla snapped. "You do not mind accepting my hospitality, living in my house for free, and eatin' the food I pay for."

"That just proves you are stupid," Tanner Lee smirked. "You seem to have no love for me, so why support me? Which you don't have to do, by the way. I make a good paycheck as a Detective and can support myself. You just want something to hold over my head so you can lord it over me."

"I will hold somethin' over your head," Carla nodded. "The toilet seat; next time you need a drink at night and cannot find the kitchen because y'all drank too much whiskey."

"Look who's talking; Miss Thirty Pack. I hear Coors is putting your portrait on all of their delivery trucks."

"That is because I am a perfect female," Carla grinned. "Not no bowlegged, knock kneed piano player wannabe like y'all."

"You wish, Lard Bag," Tanner Lee grinned. "Six more pig farmers emailed me for your diet so they can use it to fatten up their swine."

"I am not fat," Carla snapped. "Now cut the shit and help Mop Head."

"Mop Head? Did you call me Mop Head, you Moon Pie sucking pile of pig shit?" Clodagh exclaimed.

Carla made Pro wrestling legend Baron Von Raschke's sign of the claw hold, which she had previously applied to Clodagh's ribcage.

"Oh, that's what I thought," Clodagh grinned. "You're Aces with me."

"I got shit to do," Carla said. "We got a new …. thing to work on. I am gonna be busy for a while; Shifty will be in charge until I get done. Y'all have a nice day now, you hear?"

"Blow me, Fatso," Clodagh muttered.

"What was that, Patrolperson?" Carla smiled.

"I said …. to know me is to love me," Clodagh grinned.

"To know know know me, is to blow, blow, blow me," Harper sang. "The Teddy Bears," she grinned. "Old people's music."

"It's to know him, not to know me, asshole," Carla said.

"You're becoming senile like Carole," Harper said. "You remember this shitty music from the Revolutionary War. Some day you'll be sitting in your office in a diaper humming along to the Beach Bums," she grinned. "When we danced he held me tight; then he walked me home that night; all the stars were shining bright, and then he porked me," she sang. "The Crystals, right?"

"I do not know," Carla sighed. "That be nigger music," she grinned as Clarence Jackson walked by.

"Nigger? Nigger what?" he exclaimed. "You white bitches always got to run the black man down. You be up to something; what is it? I hear things."

"Okay, Buckwheat DeNiro," Harper smiled. "Tell us what you hear. I'm surprised you can hear at all, with those little ears of yours."

"Rumors," Clare said. "I am the Chief of Po-lice. You gots to keep my black ass informed. That means you, Whitey," he grinned at Carla.

"I will keep your black ass tied to my porch, you bastard," Carla said. "Best watch it, boy; there be a slave auction in Alabama next month."

Now if you be through runnin' them big lips you got, I have work to do," Carla said. "Wanna come with me?" she grinned. "I got room in the trunk of my Fairlane."

"That be one crazy white girl," Clare sighed as Carla left. "I want a report by five O'clock, Harpie."

"Kiss my ass," Harper said. "I won't be here at five O'clock, and neither will you if you don't shut the hell up and leave us alone."

"I will fire your white asses, Snowflake," Clare nodded.

"Who cares," Harper said. "We can get another job any time we want, where the Chief of Police is a human; not a Mighty Joe Young lookalike affirmative action faker like you."

"Hmmph," Clare snorted as he turned to go. "Remember; report, five O'clock."

"Fuck him," Harper muttered. "Five months from now, we'll be on our own and we won't have to put up with Chief Chitlins."

"You really hate the dude, don't you?" Clodagh said.

"Nah, we just like to break his balls," Harper said. "It's just a game we play."

"Okay, Klatu; what did you find so far?" Clodagh said to Tanner Lee.

"Nothing," Tanner Lee said. "You were too busy arguing with each other and didn't tell me what you want."

"Oh. I knew that," Clodagh said. "I need to find my father."

"The zoo is online," Tanner Lee smirked. "What species?"

"You know something? You're a real pain in the ass. I don't like that," Clodagh said.

"Like all humans, you think it's okay to insult others of your kind, but you balk when somebody does it to you. That is a personality defect humans have. You should correct that."

"Yeah, I'll be sure to write that in my notebook. His name is Brandon Peter McGuire."

"And why don't you know where he is?"

"He bailed on us and ran off with some cheap blonde whore," Clodagh said.

"Was it Carla?" Tanner Lee grinned.

"No. It was a different cheap blonde whore. Last I knew he was in Bermuda."

"Oh; that means you may come up ..... short," Tanner Lee grinned. "Bermuda shorts. Get it?"

"Yeah, I get it. Don't run down to the local comedy club for an audition. Can you find him?"

"Probably, although human men who do this cover their tracks well. What makes you think he is in Bermuda?"

"I got into his computer. There was a bunch of searches for hotels etc. in Bermuda. It's all I have so far. He cancelled all his local credit cards and bank accounts."

"And I would assume he uses a fake name," Tanner Lee said.

"Maybe. I don't know."

"That's why you are a Detective Third Grade and I am a Detective First Grade. I would use .... let's see.... human men are intolerably stupid, chronic drunkards, and always pick something easy to remember. A variation of Brandon and Peter with something added would be the likely choice. Let's see."

"He doesn't drink, which is weird for an Irishman. He does cocaine."

"A most excellent life choice," Tanner Lee smirked. "Here we are; there is a Peter Brandon Wilson registered at the Rosewood Bermuda. Very good choice; I would stay there myself if I chose to visit Bermuda. It is a five star hotel on the beach."

"What isn't on the beach in Bermuda," Clodah sighed.

"Quite a few places; they are inland. That's where the ….. rabble stays," she grinned.

"One more snide remark, and I'm going to rabble your face, big mouth. You may have some tricks you learned on Saturn, but you'll never get to use them. When you least expect it, I'll be there. Then you'll see what humans can do. And you're human; just what the fuck is so superior about you?"

"I was raised by better people than humans."

"Then kiss my ass and go back where the fuck you came from. You expect cops to take your back while you spit on them in secret because they weren't raised on fucking Pluto like you were? Let me tell you something, kiddo. You're younger than me, although you look a lot older. You keep up the bullshit attitude, and you will pay the price. Some day you might need me; and guess what. I won't be there."

"I'll make a note of that. Can you play the piano?"

"No. What the hell does that have to do with police work?"

"Nothing," Tanner Lee shrugged. "People raised by Pleiadians always have a special talent that is superior to that of their human counterparts. I am a concert pianist. What can you do?"

"Would you like to see?" Clodagh said.

"Yes; I am not talking about violence, I am talking about something special. From the looks of you, I cannot conceive of anything."

"Okay," Clodagh smiled. "We can go bowling, or we can settle this here. How much money do you have?"

"Four hundred dollars," Tanner Lee said.

"Put it up. We're going to have us a little bet." Tanner Lee put her money on the desk, and Clodagh matched her. "Now watch closely." She walked over to a plant in a vase on a table. She put a one dollar bill on the table, then covered it with the vase. She came back to Tanner Lee's desk. "See what I just did?"

"Yes. You put a dollar under that plant. So?"

"Any doubt in your little Uranus brain that there is a dollar under that plant?"

"No, there is not. What is the point of this?"

"My four hundred bucks says there is no dollar under that plant," Clodagh smiled.

"You are daffy," Tanner Lee smiled.

"Duck you. Put up or shut up. Is the dollar there or not?"

"It is there."

"Go look," Clodagh said. Tanner Lee got up and went over to the plant. She lifted it up; there was no dollar there. Clodagh scooped up the cash. "Don't you ever doubt me again," she smiled. "You ain't as smart as you think you are."

"A cheap trick," Tanner Lee said as she sat down.

"So are you," Clodagh grinned. "What room is this asshole staying in?"

"He has one of the suites," Tanner Lee said. "According to this, he paid for a year in advance. The suite costs five thousand a week. Does he have that kind of money? That is a ridiculous sum. Over a quarter of a million dollars."

"I don't know," Clodagh sighed. "There was nothing much in his computer that would lead to an income like that."

"Think," Tanner Lee said. "Any names? You said he was a cocaine user. There is big money in that drug. Perhaps he was dealing."

"I can't ….. wait a minute. One name was mentioned more than once. Bartram Edwards."

"Carla mentioned him; he is an international drug dealer who operates from America with impunity."

"How do you deal drugs with impunity?" Clodagh said.

"Easy, if you are the House Majority Whip. It is the job of the Whip to enforce the rules of decorum on the House floor during debates, etc. Sort of like a Vice Principal of a High School. Are you sure that was the name?"

"Positive. I have a copy of the hard drive. You mean a major political figure is a drug dealer?"

"Of course," Tanner Lee smiled. "Do you think a minor political figure could get away with that? The Whip knows where all the skeletons are buried. He trades knowledge of that information for immunity from his own sins."

"This is really fucked up," Clodagh sighed. "I never thought the country would turn out to be a pile of shit like this at that level. We've been played and taken over."

"And there isn't anything you can do about it," Tanner Lee smirked.

"Yes there is," Clodagh nodded. "And I am gonna show you how. Carla is on leave, but Harper is here. We will show you how to kick ass and take names. My old man is first."

"Good luck," Tanner Lee said as Clodagh stood to go. "Do you need any help?"

"You want us to take you to Bermuda? Can I trust you?"

"Yes, you can. I was just …. breaking your balls, as humans put it."

"You clear it with Harper; if she says you can be trusted, you're on. Me, I could care less who goes with us. That son of a bitch is going to wish he was never born when I get my hands on him."

"Are you going to arrest him and put him into the justice system?" Tanner Lee smiled.

"Yeah, right. Keep dreaming. What's wrong with you, anyway? Don't you know what we do?"

"I do," Tanner Lee said. "In the long run, it really doesn't matter what you do here as long as you keep it here. I am more worried about what will happen when humans try to colonize other planets."

"And what happens if they do?"

"You will be no more," Tanner Lee said, looking away. "I will fight to make sure that does not happen."

"You do that. I could care less about colonizing Mars. I just want to fuck over my old man."

Stratford Police Department

900 Longbrook Ave.

Stratford, Connecticut

June, 2008

"Bermuda?" Harper grinned. "That's almost as good as Aruba. When do we leave?"

"Half of Aruba is a toxic waste dump, thanks to Exxon. We leave in a couple of days," Clodagh said. "I have to clear it with Carla."

"She left me in charge; you clear it with me. You're cleared. There are big strong handsome dudes on that island named Rodrigo and Mateo."

"It's British," Clodagh sighed. "More likely you'll get a dude named Nigel whose sister is his Aunt."

"How could that happen?" Harper exclaimed. "I'll have to ask Lord Ashton Creighton from the WWA. He'll know."

"You pork your Aunt, who you think is your real Aunt but is really your mother. The puppy is now your sister. Get it?"

"Not really," Harper said. "I don't like British men. Can we go someplace else?"

"No. Pack your bags."

"Do I have to pay?" Harper grinned. "I only have forty dollars."

"And delicate skin," Clodagh said. "Pack some Hawaiian Tropic and sunglasses."

Rosewood Bermuda Hotel

60 Tuckers Point Drive, Hamilton Parish

Island of Bermuda

June, 2008

"Welcome to Bermuda," the desk clerk smiled. "How was your trip?"

"It took two hours, Winston," Clodagh sighed. "That hardly qualifies as a trip."

"My name is Chance," the man said. "Not Winston."

"Good thing you aren't overweight," Harper grinned. "Then your name would be Fat Chance. Get it?"

"Yes; very amusing. You should visit the Cabaret downstairs. They may need an opening act for Sir Paul."

"Who?" Clodagh said. "The King is here?"

"We have no King; only a Queen. Sir Paul McCartney is here. I assume you know who he is."

"The Deadbeatles," Harper sighed. "Old people's music. I suppose the Beach Bums are here, too. Well it's been building up inside of me for oh I don't know how long; the Metamucil didn't work so now I use some hot dog tongs…."

"Mr. Wilson will be here next week," Chance smirked. "Don't tell me you do not like the Beatles."

"Okay, we won't tell you," Harper said. "We weren't even born when they were popular. That McCartney dude is older than dirt."

"As you wish; the tickets are three hundred dollars American if you change your mind."

"She loves me, yeah yeah, yeah, she loves me yeah, yeah, yeah, she loves me yeah, yeah, yeah, yeah," Harper sang. "Bet it took him all month to write that one, huh, Skippy?"

"I will summon a porter to take your bags to your suite," Chance smiled. "I will relay the fact that you will not be attending Sir Paul's concert. I'm sure he'll be crushed."

The porter came, and they headed for the elevators.

"That desk dude is hilarious," Clodagh said. "That's what they call dry humor, right, Miss Britannica?"

"How astute of you to notice," Tanner Lee smirked.

"I'm not a Stute; I'm Irish," Clodagh said. "You didn't book us like next door to my old man, did you, E.T.?"

"No," Tanner Lee said. "He is on the other side of the hotel on the top floor."

"Good. That's the fifth floor. That will do."

"For what?" Tanner Lee laughed.

"Hey; shit happens," Clodagh shrugged. "People become despondent and jump out the window, or they get drunk and fall off a balcony."

Rosewood Bermuda Hotel

60 Tuckers Point Drive, Hamilton Parish

Island of Bermuda

June, 2008

"I don't ever want to leave here," Harper grinned. "This place is top shelf. The food is great, the liquor is the best, and the rooms we have are to die for. And the best part is I'm not paying."

"So I noticed, cheapskate," Clodagh said. "We can't stay here on my dime forever, you know. This place is expensive."

"Oh, come on; I'm sure they have a bowling alley here. You can hustle somebody to pay for the bill."

"The staff is British," Clodagh grinned. "The guy who brings our room service orders has a big scar on his neck where they removed his second head. And he only has four teeth. Brits don't bowl."

"Nobody is perfect," Harper said. "The beach here is divine. I want to work on my tan."

"You're Scottish; you don't have a tan. You go on the beach here and you'll look like a pop tart inside of half an hour. It's closer to the equator, and the sun is brutal."

"Excuses, excuses. I bet we can order some Swedish dudes to give us massages and hand jobs."

"It's Bermuda, not Jeff Epstein's teenage hooker ranch. They have class here; there is no Rub Me the Wrong Way Massage Parlor in the concourse."

"Well there should be," Harper snapped. "How is a girl supposed to pleasure herself here?"

"You aren't," Clodagh said. "Unless you get lucky with the garbage man."

"Is he cute?" Harper grinned.

"Just stop, okay? As soon as I complete my mission, we're out of here."

"That's the thanks I get for backing you up," Harper grumbled. "I risk my hide coming down here and you want to deprive me of a couple of days vacation?"

"Yeah. There will be an investigation after my old man is …. you know. It would be best if we were not here."

"We used fake names," Harper said. "We won't be suspects."

"Only if the cops here are as smart as Carla," Clodagh grinned.

"I'm telling," Harper huffed. "You insulted the future Chief of Police in Lordship."

"It won't be the first time I insulted her, and it won't be the last. She can take a flying fuck at a rolling donut if she doesn't like it. This has nothing to do with her, or police work. It is a vendetta; I'm sure she'd approve if she could spell vendetta."

"Martha and the Vendettas," Harper nodded. "More old people's music."

"Oh, good morning, ladies," Sir Paul McCartney smiled as he got into the elevator.

"Good morning," Harper smiled. "It's him," she whispered to Clodagh. "Sir what's his name from the Deadbeatles."

"Tally Ho, old man," Clodagh smiled, and curtsied. "Although we aren't hos."

"I see," Paul smiled as he hummed Eleanor Rigby. "You're Americans, right?"

"Yes," Harper said. "What gave us away? The unfamiliar smell of soap, or the straight teeth?"

"No British accent," Paul smiled. "May I see your teeth? I usually look when I purchase a horse."

"Oh my God!" Clodagh shrieked. "He got you there, Flicka."

"I beg your pardon," Harper said. "I know who you are. Our boss likes you; she's almost as old as you are. We, on the other hand, and watch your hands, are not."

"I see," Paul smiled. "Not everyone likes my music, or the Beatles' music. Musical education is not what it used to be."

"Neither are you," Harper snickered. "No offense, Paul; it's just that your stuff is …. well, passé. The people who listen to the Beatles are mostly in rest homes. You're next."

"Perhaps," Paul shrugged as the elevator door slid open. "I do enjoy performing for my fans, though. It keeps me young. Cheers," he smiled as he headed for his suite.

"If singing that crap keeps you young, It didn't do a very good job," Harper muttered.

"You just can't resist it, can you," Tanner Lee sighed. "Ridiculing a music legend. They listen to the Beatles in the Pleiadian Star System."

"Now I know what's wrong with you," Harper said. "Let's get this over with."

"You guys wait here," Clodagh said as the elevator door opened. "Keep the security busy, if they even have any, which I doubt. This won't take long; we'll go downstairs and have dinner when I'm done, then we're out of here."

"I don't have to pay for dinner, do I?" Harper grinned.

"Why break a tradition?" Clodagh smiled. She headed for the door to her father's suite. She put her ear to the door; the only sound was the distant running of a shower. The door was unlocked. She let herself in; there was nobody in sight. A woman's handbag was on the coffee table; she looked around and peeked into the second bedroom. A blonde was snoring away on the bed. Clodagh wedged the door shut with a rubber block and opened the sliding glass door leading to the balcony, then snuck over to the bathroom.

She pushed the door open a few inches; the shower enclosure had a mottled glass door which would prevent the occupant from seeing who had just entered. She waited for the water to stop, then pushed the glass door open, her Glock up and ready.

"Hi, Daddy," she grinned. "Guess who. Dry off and get dressed."

"What the ….. Clodagh? How did you find me?" Brandon exclaimed.

"I found you because I'm a Stratford cop now, and you're a no good asshole. Any more questions?"

"I'm not wanted for any crime," Brandon said as he grabbed a towel. "Even if I was, you don't have jurisdiction here."

"You're wanted for a different type of crime; now get dressed. And never mind the bullshit excuses like it's not your fault you were fucking Bambi in there while we were wondering where our next meal was coming from."

"It isn't," Brandon said as he put on his clothes.

"Sure," Clodagh smiled. "Just like it isn't your fault you're shacked up with the same blonde whore you used to email and talk to on the phone when you thought nobody was home. I was home; and I listened in on your conversations. Oh; by the way, I just killed her," Clodagh lied.

"What? You killed Ronnie? I don't believe you."

"Who cares what you believe. Come with me; and don't try any bullshit, or I will make you wish you were never born. Remember the Israeli dude? He taught me how to fight. Now fucking move it. Out on the deck, and stay there. I have to raid your computer before I take you back home."

Fifteen minutes later, Clodagh left a note on the table and removed the rubber block from the blonde's door. She left the suite with her father's laptop and nodded at Harper.

"Done," she said. "Let's go."

Stratford Police Department

900 Longbrook Ave.

Stratford, Connecticut

June, 2008

"Where were you three?" Carole said.

"Personal time," Clodagh said. "Vacation in Bermuda. Why?"

"There is a story on the international wire about some dude who jumped off a fifth floor balcony in Bermuda. He was registered as Peter Brandon."

"That's nice," Clodagh said. "What does that have to do with us?"

"Your father's name was Brandon Peter McGuire."

"And your point would be?"

"The British authorities are investigating."

"That's nice of them," Clodagh smiled. "I know what you're thinking; forget it. We were on vacation, not a murder spree."

"I didn't authorize personal time for you."

"Nobody asked you to," Harper said. "I am acting Chief of D in Carla's absence. I authorized it."

"Acting?" Carole smirked. "Some act. You three disappear without saying a word, and creep face's daddy is found splattered all over a parking lot."

"What evidence do they have that he was my ….. daddy?" Clodagh smiled.

"None, yet. His fingers and feet were burned so badly they couldn't get prints, all his teeth were yanked out, and he landed face first so a positive ID is impossible. There was also a suicide note left on the table. How he typed that with no fingers is beyond me. Good work."

"A lot of things are beyond you," Harper nodded. "Like justice, for starters. Oh; we met Sir Paul McCartney in the elevator. He was there to do a concert with the Metamucil Brothers and the Preparation H Project."

"You met Paul McCartney?" Carole swooned. "How does he look?"

"Old," Harper grinned. "He should iron his face or get plastic surgery."

"He is one of the most important figures in pop music history," Carole snapped.

"And your point would be? Were we supposed to be dazzled by his presence? Would you be dazzled if Jose Carreras walked in here?" Harper said.

"Who?" Carole said. "Is he an illegal alien?"

"I rest my case," Harper said. "Let's go, girls. It's time for Carole's nap."

Stratford Police Department

900 Longbrook Ave.

Stratford, Connecticut

June, 2008

"Okay, Martian Millie, let's find Rollie's asshole father. She thinks he's in Bermuda," Clodagh said.

"Seems to be the place to go when you bail on your wife," Tanner Lee sighed. "We just came back from there. We should be careful."

"Fuck careful," Clodagh said. "The dude needs to pay the price. Besides, we need to find his dough. It's in Nevis."

"See Carla; she's been there a couple of times," Tanner Lee said.

"She isn't here," Harper said. "I am. I was in Nevis with her. Vito went with us. Look for him, Sis," Harper said.

"Let me do a check." Tanner Lee typed in a few commands on the computer, and sat back. "Nobody with the last name of Randall is registered in any Bermuda hotel. What is his first name?" Tanner Lee sighed.

"Richard," Rollie said. "He's a real dick," she giggled.

Tanner Lee ran the name and all variations.

"How about Randall Richards?" she smiled. "I got a hit on a Visa credit card. A restaurant in San Francisco, California. Trattorina Cucina Italiano."

"He's in California?" Rollie said.

"Maybe. That could be a popular name, very common sounding."

"Check the DMV database," Harper said. Tanner Lee got into the database.

"Here is a Randall Richards in Alameda, California." She hit the printer and handed the printout of the license to Rollie.

"That's him," Rollie nodded.

"You say Alameda, I say Ala-myda, let's call the whole thing off," Harper sang.

"Shut up, Twisted Sister," Tanner Lee sighed. "He has a license issued in one city but used his credit card in San Francisco. That's 21 miles away, across the bay. You have to take the ferry."

"He's not gay," Rollie said. "He'd take a girl."

"Good grief," Tanner Lee sighed. "I'm surrounded by idiots. Lots of people go to San Fran-Sicko to dine out or go to the theater. Maybe they can verify it's him."

"I wouldn't eat anything from that city," Clodagh huffed. "It's full of queers. You could get AIDS eating there."

"Depends on what you like to eat," Tanner Lee smirked. "Humans are liable to do most anything, especially if it involves their tongue. That is why your dirty planet has been quarantined by the Supreme Council."

"Fuck your Supreme Council," Clodagh said. "We know all about your little program to monitor us. One wrong move, and Sammy from Saturn will zap us, is that it?"

"There are no colonies on Saturn," Tanner Lee said. "It will not support life. The Council is located in the Pleiadian Star System. Best watch out," she grinned. "They know who's been naughty and nice. Let's get back to Richard. He used his credit card at the Happy Traveler Motel, too."

"You're kidding," Harper said. "We've been thrown out of those motels more times than we can count. What would he be doing there?"

"Oooooooh, baby!" Rollie cried as she leaned back and writhed in her chair, her legs in the air. "Give it to me! You're the best piece of ass I had since my sister!"

"There's an image I could do without," Tanner Lee said.

"You haven't met my old man," Rollie said. "He'd nail a snake if it stood still."

"Charming. It seems the human male doesn't have the capability of being faithful to its chosen mate."

Harper took a picture of the local AT&T supervisor's wife from her bag and showed it to Tanner Lee. "Any more questions?" she smiled.

"Good God, is that a human?" Tanner Lee exclaimed. "Now I understand. Even you would be a better choice than that creature, and you are a short haired stunted midget."

"Thank you," Harper smiled. "Don't go to sleep tonight if you know what's good for you."

"Get thee to California and leave me alone," Tanner Lee sighed. "I need my rest."

"From what? You don't do anything. Saddle up, motherfucker," Harper grinned. "You are about to find out what it's like to be on the road with me and Vito."

"What about me?" Rollie said.

"You can tag along as ballast. You're a civilian; we cannot expose you to danger."

"Deputize me," Rollie nodded. "That way when I kill that cocksucker I can claim self defense."

"Girl knows her law," Harper nodded. "Raise your paw, Junior."

Trattorina Cucina Italiano

1700 Mason St.

San Francisco, California

June, 2008

"Good God, Vito, you stink something awful," Tanner Lee sighed as she rolled down her window.

"Shaddup, Slag," Vito grinned. "I smell like a real man."

"A real dead man," Tanner Lee sighed as they pulled into the restaurant parking lot.

"This is the best Guinea restaurant in town," Vito grinned. "I know; I got this straight from Don Pasta Lasagna. He knows."

"Sure," Harper said as they got out. She saw a small Japanese flag in the window, but said nothing. "I'm sure these are real Italians," she grinned.

"You bet they are," Vito nodded as they went inside. A girl came over.

"Want table? This man smell bad," she said, backing away from Vito. "Have to sit in shit house."

"Youse ain't no Guinea," Vito said when he saw her obvious Asian face. "Youse is a faker, hired by real Italians. That ain't so bad," he shrugged. "Even Japs got to work. Give us a table."

"Over here," the girl said, holding her nose. "Away from people. Waiter come soon."

A waiter came over; he was wearing sunglasses. "Yo, like Paisan," he grinned as he read from an index card. "Youse want to order?"

"What's with the shades?" Vito said.

"Have Cadillacs," the waiter grinned. "Light bother eyes. Need surgery."

"Yeah, just like the flash over Hero-sheeny bothered your eyes," Vito grinned. "I want Lasagna and real Guinea Antipasto, real Guinea wine, Italian bread, and pizza with anchovies."

"Girls?" the waiter said as he wrote.

"We'll have the same," Harper said. "We want Polish Blackberry Brandy."

"No have Polack work here," the waiter said. "This Italian restaurant."

"The brandy is Polish, you moron!" Harper yelled. "Yellow and red label. Leroux. You bring anything else and we will take you outside and kill you," she smiled. "Caprice?"

"Okay, I bring," the waiter shrugged. "Why this man smell like poopy?" he said, eyeing Vito. "Him step in dog shit?"

"There ain't no dogs around here," Vito grinned. "Youse dinks had 'em all for lunch."

"What do we get to drink, you lush?" Clodagh said.

"Kool-Aid," Harper snapped. "You aren't old enough to drink liquor."

"Oh, I see. I'm old enough to blow up underground cities and waste the Kamatos Family and their boys, but I can't order a drink?"

"That's right," Harper said. "We aren't in Connecticut."

"Okay," Clodagh shrugged. She waved for the sommelier, who looked like Mao Tse Tung.

"Yes, Missy?" he grinned.

"Bring me a quart of Jameson's Irish Whiskey and two glasses, Tojo," Clodagh said.

"Have to see ID."

"Okay, come with me," Clodagh smiled. She took the boy into an alcove; several horrible screams ensued. Clodagh came back out and waved at the other patrons. "No problem," she smiled. "He fell down and hurt his penis." She sat back down. The sommelier appeared a minute later with the Jameson's; he was sweating and clutching his groin. He gave Clodagh a mean look.

"What's with the bad eye?" Clodagh said. "You're down one nut; care to go for two?"

"No, Missy," the boy cried. "You enjoy drink."

"Damn straight, you gook bastard," Clodagh nodded as she filled two glasses and gave one to Rollie. "Anybody else got anything to say?" she grinned as she sat back in her chair.

"Youse is a psycho kid," Vito grinned. "And this other Diaper Dolly don't look no better than you."

"Diaper Dolly?" Rollie grinned as she gulped her Jameson's. "Who the fuck are you to judge me, Mr. Stinky? Walk a mile in my shoes and see what it's like. You're Italian; you believe in tradition, family, and a great culture of food, music, and religion. Tell me I'm wrong."

"Youse is right," Vito said.

"Then why can't I have the same thing?" Rollie yelled. "So I'm not Italian. Don't I deserve a good life? I'm a fucking teenager!" she screamed as everybody in the restaurant looked at her. "I never asked for what happened to me! My old man dumped us and ran off with a whore! You tell me I can't have a good life."

The patrons all stood up and applauded. Vito looked around and nodded.

"Okay, I didn't mean youse is like inferiorated. Kids should have a good life."

"Then you back me," Rollie said. "I'll fix my own fucking problem. I need to know you are behind me."

"Youse got it, kid," Vito nodded. "The whole department backs you."

"Just don't get caught," Harper giggled as she slurped her Brandy. "Hey; I don't have to pay for this dinner, do I?"

"Of course not," Tanner Lee said as she grabbed the Jameson's and filled her water glass. "Why would we change the rules after ten years?"

"We wouldn't," Harper said. "You drunken bastard."

"Look who's talking," a fat woman at the next table said. "Could you possibly keep your big mouths shut over there? You're interrupting my dinner."

"I'll take this," Clodagh smiled. "So, Shamu, it doesn't look like anybody has interrupted your dinner since you were a baby calf in Mommy's barn. What's your beef, other than the five pound roast you had for lunch?"

"Why you little rat," the woman hissed. "Do you know who I am?"

"Miss Butterbutt 2008?" Clodagh grinned.

"I am the Mayor of San Francisco's wife," the woman hissed. "Francine Delwood."

"Oh; I guess that makes it all right for you to insult us. Do you know who we are?"

"No, I do not."

Harper kicked Clodagh under the table. "We're just tourists," she smiled.

"Then you should shut your mouths and give me the respect I deserve," Francine snapped.

"Do you have a halter?" Clodagh grinned. "I can use it to lead you to your trough, you fat bastard."

"Here we go," Harper sighed. "Why does this always happen to us?"

"What did you call me?" Francine screeched. "I will have you arrested for that!"

"Not likely," Clodagh said as she got up and went over to the fat woman. She grabbed the woman's bag, took out her phone, and threw it into the fireplace. "Who are you going to call now; Fatbusters?"

"You ugly red headed bastard!" Francine screeched. "Antonio! Come here at once!"

"Yes, Missy?" Antonio said as he came over.

"Call the police."

"Yes, Missy," Antonio said as he bowed. Vito grabbed him on the way to the back.

"Yo, Guinea faker," he smiled as he stuck his .45 in Antonio's face. "Youse ain't Italian. I am. Youse can be arrested for imitating a Guinea. That's a federal crime. Youse want to do ten years?"

"No!" Antonio said. "The boss say to use this name."

"Okay; youse go outside and have a smoke. Don't touch no phones, or else."

Inside, Francine looked around. "It won't be long now," she nodded. "You're going to jail."

"I don't think so," Clodagh smiled. "Care to settle this the old fashioned way?"

"And what would that be?" Francine said.

"Eating contest," Clodagh grinned. "You against Audrey."

"Me against that skinny little thing?" Francine laughed. "You have to be kidding. I had more than her for breakfast."

"Opinions vary," Clodagh said. "What say you, Audrey?"

"I can beat her," Harper said. "You want to take me on, Blubber Butt?"

"You're on," Francine nodded. "What's the bet?"

"If I win, you forget we were ever here and divorce your gay husband," Harper grinned. "If you win, we pay you ten thousand dollars. Or at least she will," Harper said, pointing at Clodagh. I only have forty dollars."

"You're on, Shrimp. And my husband isn't gay."

"Oh, no?" Tanner Lee smiled as she took out a set of photographs taken by a private investigator. They showed Francine's husband in a series of compromising positions with another man. "Explain these."

"Those have to be fake!" Francine screeched. "He likes women!"

"But not you," Tanner Lee smiled. "The only resemblance between you and a woman is …. well, there is none. Live with it. Let the eating begin. You can't please a man, perhaps you can win an eating contest. You may have finally been challenged to do something you are good at."

"You bastards," Francine hissed. "You want this? You got it. I want Ziti and meatballs."

"I'll take the same for a starter," Harper smiled. "There is an old saying; sometimes you just can't help yourself, and you pick on the wrong person. Say hello to the wrong person."

"Half an hour later, Francine conceded. "I don't believe you ate all that," she sighed.

"You want the rest of that pizza?" Harper said.

"Take it. I'm leaving; I never saw you here, whoever you are." She struggled to her feet and lumbered off.

"She won't say anything," Clodagh said. "She doesn't know who we are, and we sure as hell aren't going to leave anybody around who does."

"Youse gonna whack your old man?" Vito grinned, eyeing Rollie.

"Who, me?" Rollie grinned. "I'd never do anything like that. I'm just a kid."

"Youse is the devil with pigtails," Vito said. "I been working with kids like you since Carla showed up here in 1994. Youse is all mentally decapitated and got a screw loose."

"How dare you impugn our character," Harper huffed as she finished Francine's pizza. "We are honest people."

"Youse is loony bird whackos," Vito said. "And Little Beelzebub ovadere ain't no different."

"Ovadere?" Rollie giggled. "What's ovadere?"

"You, stunod," Vito said. "That's Guinea for stupid, which I ain't and youse is."

"Vito speaks his own language," Harper said. "It takes some getting used to."

"So does his body odor," Clodagh muttered. "Some day when he least expects it, he's going to get a good steam cleaning and some deodorant."

"Youse ain't gonna do nothing to me," Vito said. "No broad is gonna wash my junk or spray me with that girly fag perfume. I'm a real man; I use alcohol on my pits. If that ain't good enough for you, too friggin' bad."

"Can we talk about something else?" Harper said. "I just ate. I have a dainty appetite and a soft stomach."

"Youse got a soft skull," Vito beamed. "Youse just ate enough ziti to feed a small town. That ain't dainty."

"Yes it is," Harper said as she emitted a frog-like belch. "Excuse me," she grinned. "See? I have manners, too."

"You seem to forget why we came here," Tanner Lee gurgled.

"So you could get pie-eyed on Irish whiskey?" Harper said.

"That, and we have to see if Rollie's soon to be late father ate here."

"Who cares," Harper said with a wave of her hand. She grabbed a Cannoli off the desert tray, dunked it in her brandy, and ate it. "What difference does it make?"

"We have to make sure we waste the right person, dipshit," Clodagh said. "He could have bribed somebody at the DMV, like that would be a surprise, and had a license made with some other dude's picture."

"Oh," Harper said as she bolted another Cannoli. "Killing the right person should have some priority," she smiled. "Wasting some shlub who doesn't know why we did it is impolite."

"Glad to see you're using those manners you claim to have. Give it up; me and Rollie will do it." Harper handed over the license printout. "Come on, Rollie. Time to learn the first rule of being an undercover cop."

"What's that?" Rollie said.

"Never tell them your real name." They went over to a hallway that lead to an office. A big man stepped in front of them.

"Ladies' room is over there," he nodded.

"Police," Clodagh said, flashing her badge quickly. "We want to see the owner for a minute."

"Wait here." The man knocked on the door and went inside. He came back a minute later. "Make it quick. The boss is busy."

They went inside. "Inspector Lolly Popp, with two Ps. No jokes, either," Clodagh said.

"Awful young to be a cop, ain't you?" the big Italian said. His nameplate simply said "Dom."

"Yeah; so what? What's with all the gooks working in a Guinea restaurant?"

"It's friggin' San Francisco," Dom laughed. "Half the damn city is gooks. Chinks, Japs, Koreans; who gives a shit. The other half is fags. You take what you can get for help. This is a good gig," he shrugged. "Them gay dudes got money. Whaddaya want? I got shit to do."

"Ever see this guy in here?" Clodagh said, holding up the picture.

"Yeah; he comes here a lot."

"Alone?"

"Nah, he got a bracciole with him. Redhead with big hair, a lot of flash, high heels, and tight bodysuits."

"My God, he's fucking Peggy Bundy," Rollie sighed.

"Yeah," Dom grinned. "Looks just like her. I remember him because he's about the only guy who comes in here with a woman. He wanted by the cops?"

"We can't discuss that," Clodagh said. "You might fold under pressure," she grinned. "Got a credit card receipt? We need his address." Dom just stared at her. "Jesus, you fucking Dagos are all alike." She dropped two C-notes on the floor. "Finders keepers."

"Now that's what I call a good cop," Dom grinned as he opened a filing cabinet.

Residence of "Randall Richards"

895 West Avenue Drive

Alameda, California

June, 2008

"Good location," Harper whispered. "Last house on a dead end street."

"Dead end," Rollie grinned. "I like that term. I'm going to give it a new meaning for Pops."

"Okay, there aren't many neighbors, and their houses are dark. They probably went to bed. Clo-dog, you go right. I'll go left. Vito, you can go fuck yourself," Harper grinned.

"Youse maniacs is gonna do a hit on this poor son of a bitch. Maybe I should go back to the fake Guinea restaurant."

"I knew we could depend on you," Harper sighed.

They snuck up to the house. Vito, who had relented and went up the middle, peeked in a living room window. Randall was lying on a sofa watching TV. He pointed at the window and made a "TV" sign with his fingers. Rollie went around back; the door was unlocked. She let herself in and screwed a silencer onto an untraceable nine millimeter pistol. She stood behind the entryway to the living room and took aim.

"Hi, Pop," she said softly. Randall looked up; he saw the gun, and his life flashed before his eyes. Rollie put an end to the vision by putting a Glaser Safety Slug between Randall's eyes. The effect was quite dramatic and messy. Rollie, who was wearing surgical gloves, put Randall's prints on the gun and dropped it next to the sofa. She then went through the dead man's desk until she found bank records. She locked the door on her way out.

"That was fast," Harper said as they headed for the car.

"Well, we aren't getting paid by the hour," Rollie said. "Let's go home."

The Orion Motorcar Company

Lordship Boulevard

Stratford, Connecticut

June, 2008

"Oh, it's you," Christine Connor smiled when Harper came in. "The wrestler. How are you?"

"Fine," Harper said. "Yourself?"

"I'm better than I deserve," Christine smiled. "Or so some people say. What's this?" she said, pointing at Clodagh.

"This is Detective Clodagh McGuire."

"Oh, hello, Chloe," Christine said.

"It's Clodagh. Clooooo-dah. Got it?" Clodagh said.

"Odd Irish name, but not hard to pronounce. Sit down and be quiet."

"What did you say?" Clodagh laughed.

"You heard me," Christine said. "Do I stutter?"

"Oh, this broad is cruising for a bruising," Clodagh nodded as she sat down. "What's your problem?"

"Insolent little teenagers who don't yet know their place," Christine said. "I know; I used to be one."

"Doesn't look like you made much of an improvement," Clodagh said.

"I own a multi billion dollar automobile company," Christine said. "What do you own?"

"Your ass, if you don't knock it off," Clodagh said.

"You think so?" Christine said. "I told you to sit there and be quiet," she said, her dead eyes boring into Clodagh's as she leaned across her desk. Clodagh held Christine's gaze for a minute, then looked away. "That's better," Christine said. "Now … why are you here, Humper?" she smiled.

"Oh, you're a riot, you are," Harper laughed. "I thought you should meet Clo-dog; she's going to be working next door come December when we open the new police department."

"You said November," Harper said.

"Too much bullshit going on around here. December looks better."

"So Clumsy Dog will be my neighbor? Lucky me," Christine smirked.

"Oh, and Clo-dog called you a whack job." Harper said.

"That just means …." Clodagh began.

"I know what it means," Christine said. "It is a most insulting term. It suggests that I have some sort of mental defect. I assure you, I do not."

"Jeez, lady, ease up, okay? It's just a little dig, okay?"

"Fine. Now that I've met ….. Clo-dog, you may remove her from my office," Christine smiled at Harper. "It doesn't appear that there is any further reason for me to attempt to have a conversation with such a disrespectful little urchin."

"Urchin?" Cldaogh exclaimed. "You called me an urchin? What the hell is an urchin?"

"A mischievous young child," Christine smirked. "That would be you, although you do not look like a child; you just act like one. You haven't learned how to show respect to people who have accomplished far more than you ever will. That would be me."

"Oh, I see," Clodagh said. "You build cars. I carry a badge and a gun. Who has more power?"

"I do, because I pay your salary," Christine said. "Your badge and gun mean only one thing here; you have taken an oath to protect me and my property. How do you like that? If it requires you to lay down your life for me, you will do so."

"She's right," Harper nodded. "That's the job, whether you like it or not."

"Horse shit," Clodagh said. "I'm not putting my ass on the line for her."

"Well now," Christine said, sitting back. "Harper is a Chief; you are not. You just refused to do your job according to your oath. What are you going to do about that, Harper? I suggest you take her badge and fire her."

"No!" Clodagh exclaimed. "You can't fire me! Not over that," she said.

"Yes I can," Harper grinned. "Christine lives here, for better or worse, and we swore to protect her. What do you have to say now?"

"All right," Clodagh sighed. "I'll do it. As if she needs it. Who the hell would want to kill her?"

"Lots of people," Christine said. "We own forty percent of the luxury car market through Monarch. Nobody can compete with us. We've had offers over the last few years you wouldn't believe; our competitors want to buy us out for twice what Monarch is worth. When I turn them down, I get death threats."

"Why not take the deal?" Clodagh shrugged. "You could retire."

"I could have retired ten years ago. We won't sell because our company is worth more to us than money. It is what we do; it is what we are. The people who would purchase Monarch would have our blueprints sent to China or some other third world hell hole and have our cars built accordingly, but with half the quality and a trick warranty. Do you see how it works in this world?" Christine smiled. "Quality means nothing; profit is the only goal, at any cost. They would take the Monarch name and grind it into obscurity through their trickery and deceit while they profit billions. We will not allow that."

"I never saw one of your cars," Clodagh said. "Are they that good?"

"They beat Rolls-Royce, Bentley, Mercedes, Jaguar, and Maserati hands down in every independent evaluation. You probably never saw one because nobody in this town can afford one. The property taxes here are too high," Christine smiled, eyeing Harper.

"Hey; don't look at me. I don't set the mill rate," Harper said.

"How did you get started?" Clodagh said.

"My father began his quest working in Maldonado's junkyard as a very young man; he got a job at Monarch from that effort, and now he owns the company because the founder, Barclay Wells, saw the same drive in my father that he had; the desire to achieve, to be the best there is in your chosen field. My father lives by that standard; so do I. I will never sell or surrender my company, and my father will never surrender his. Those who don't like it can learn to live with it."

"But you said you get death threats," Clodagh said.

"Yes, but I pay them no mind. Although I do take basic precautions; I have a beautiful suite above the factory; I stay here, rather than commuting back and forth to Pleasantville. This is standard procedure in business; those who cannot beat you in the free market threaten to kill you. They never try, of course, because they are incompetent nincompoops. If they cannot build a better car than me, how would they muster the mental acumen to have me killed?"

"I could whack you," Clodagh shrugged. "What if I was on the take and General Motors paid me to get rid of you?"

"Would you do it?" Christine smiled. "Do you have the low character that an assassin would require? A desire for money that would let you sell the last shred of character you possess and commit murder for hire? Would you do that?"

"No," Clodagh sighed, looking down. "I wouldn't do murder for hire. But you better pray I never change my mind, because I'd get you within twenty four hours."

"She just whacks people for free," Harper smiled.

"You shut the hell up about that!" Clodagh yelled. "She's just kidding," she smiled. "I'd never do that."

"I don't care if you do or not," Christine said. "That's between you and whatever force of nature you feel obligated to account to."

"What makes you think there is one?" Clodagh said, sitting back. "You think I have a conscience or something?"

"You work for Carla," Christine said. "Of course you have a conscience. She would not have hired you otherwise."

"Do you have one?" Clodagh said.

"Yes, but mine is based in reason and logic, not religious fantasy."

"Reason, huh? What's that?"

"The power of the mind to analyze one's life and take the actions necessary to achieve personal happiness independent of criticism, coercion, government regulation, or religious fantasy. That is man's highest logical goal; his own happiness."

"At whose expense?" Clodagh said.

"Nobody's; your happiness is your own burden. You do not have the right to achieve it at the expense of your fellow man, no more than you would have him achieve his at your expense. Don't you see how it works? It's really very simple. Every man for himself, minus coercion or government interference. Every man sells what he has in the free market to other free men, for mutual value. Nothing could be more simple.”

“Carla hooks pussy,” Clodagh grinned. “You think that’s part of the free market?”

“Only an insolent twit with a low IQ like yours would actually believe her stories. They are largely a product of her imagination, designed to entertain.”

“So you say. What if they really are true?” Clodagh said.

“Prove they are,” Christine smirked. “Or charge her publicly, and see what happens to you after that.”

“Hey,” Clodagh said, holding up her hands. “I may be stupid, but I’m not crazy. I’ve seen first hand what she can do.”

“Then drop it,” Christine said. “You seem to be a bright young person, despite your nasty mouth and lack of respect for your betters. Would you like to come to work for me for a week or two and find out just how smart you really are?”

“Nope. I have a job. Besides, I don’t know anything about cars.”

“Or life, or morality, or philosophy, or anything else of much value. Man survives by virtue of his mind; he has no other protection. You know how to kill, and don’t ask me how I know. That is a skill the lowest creatures on Earth possess; they use it for survival, however, not revenge. Where does that place you?” Christine smiled. “Above, or below the animals?”

“What the hell is that supposed to mean?” Clodagh exclaimed. “There are a lot of people around here who don’t deserve to be alive.”

“Oh, come on,” Christine laughed. “I’ve been through this with Carla; don’t tell me she trained you to be her personal executioner in absentia. She does claim to be God’s personal avenger, you know.”

“Prove she isn’t.”

“I don’t have to; I didn’t make the claim. Have her prove it.”

“I can’t. There is no way to prove something like that. Besides, she’s a good person.”

“I agree; for today, anyway. I warned her about her proclivities; she could have some sort of mental breakdown, and then what? Who would God’s avenger kill then? You? Me? Some old lady on the street walking home with her groceries she perceives to be a threat sparked by some paranoid delusion?”

“She would never do that,” Clodagh said.

“I see. She only kills the better class of felons, and you will follow in her footsteps. Notice I said will; there is no reasoning with a person like you; there is no reach of the intelligent mind that can connect with what lurks in your skull. And you,” she said, eyeing Harper. “You aren’t any better. You should be ashamed of yourself polluting this young person’s mind.”

“I didn’t do anything wrong,” Harper pouted. “She was already a miserable, murdering bastard when we hired her.”

“Cute. Just what this town needs; we don’t have enough criminals, we have to add some to our police force.”

"Hey look, Chrissy," Harper smiled. "You had Carla work here and she quit after one day. Now you want Douche Bag Junior to work for you so you can shove her around and show her how smart you are. We know how smart you are with a wrench in your hand. How about you take your own challenge?"

"Doing what?" Christine laughed. "Work in my own plant? Everyone here knows I can perform every function required to build a car. I built them with my own hands since I was fifteen."

"I mean my challenge. Put on a uniform and carry a badge. Go out into Stratford and enforce the law with your reason and logic."

"I could do it," Christine said. "But I prefer to pay you to do it instead."

"You're a rich little coward," Harper said. "You like to have people protect you because you have money, but when it comes down to us against the bad guys, you'll hide under your bed and let us do the dirty work; then you'll criticize us for the way we do it. We know how to do it; you don't. I don't need any lectures from you; I go out on those streets every day to protect the people in this town, and I do it the way I see fit. If you don't like it, strap on a gun and ride a cruiser."

"Is that what you'd like to see?" Christine smiled. "I know the law, and I am an excellent shot with a pistol. I could do what you do."

"Prove it, big mouth," Harper said. "Get your old man to come down here and run this place for a few days; I'll teach you about crime in Stratford."

"All right; I'll do it. I've never had a challenge I couldn't meet," Christine smiled.

"First time for everything," Harper smiled. "Report to Chief Antonelli Monday morning. You're going on patrol."

"I'll be there," Christine said. "Now if that's all you want, I have work to do."

Outside, Clodagh turned to Harper. "You think she'll show up?"

"Sure," Harper shrugged. "Miss Invincible Car Robot who has never been proven wrong in her life wants to be a cop. Let's see how that works out for her."

"I know who you're going to send her out there with," Clodagh grinned.

"Yeah," Harper sighed. "Not too hard to figure that one out, was it."

Stratford Police Department

900 Longbrook Ave.

Office of Chief of Patrol Vito Antonelli

Stratford Police Department

900 Longbrook Ave.

June, 2008

"Yo, Sweet Cheeks," Vito grinned when Christine came in. "I remember you. Here; go change."

"I have to wear this?" Christine exclaimed as Vito handed her a uniform. "Who made this? Versaci? Gucci?"

"Low bidder; some chink in Gookland. How the hell should I know? What, it's the wrong size?"

"No, but it's a bit too obvious, isn't it? You aren't wearing one."

"That's because I'm a Chief," Vito said. "Not no street jockey chasing speeders. I done that; not no more. I been a cop forty years; I started in New York City, and made Detective of Narcotics. What did youse ever make besides convertibles and limousines?"

"I and my father employ thousands of people with good paying jobs. I'm a businesswoman, not a cop."

"Then why are you here?" Vito said as he opened a pizza. "Have a slice."

"No thank you. I watch my figure."

"Might as well; ain't nobody else watching it. Youse is a snappy dish, as my old man would say, but youse got no ring on your finger. Why? Because youse is miserable, or youse is on the Lesbian side of town?" Vito grinned.

"I am not a Lesbian," Christine said. "It's just that after being exposed to idiotic macho men like you, I decided to stay single."

"Hey, I ain't never exposed nothing," Vito nodded. "Especially my junk. That's an infamnia. You show your stuff to kids or women, you got to be put away."

"I can see how this is going to work out. Your mental capacity hasn't increased since the last time I talked to you."

"Hey, it is what it is," Vito shrugged. "Go ahead, Cutie," he grinned. "Have a slice. All cops eat pizza. You go out on your shift, you never know if youse is coming home at night. Might as well die with a full stomach."

"Well, as long as you put it that way, I will have one slice. At least there's one left, which is a miracle considering Carole is in the building."

"She's right behind you, too," Vito beamed.

"Oh, hello, Carole," Christine smiled. "Nice to see that there is so much more of you than there was the last time."

"Why you miserable, creepy ….. are you calling me fat?" Carole exclaimed.

"No; just corpulent," Christine said.

"Oh; that's better. Corpulent is just below Sergeant. I hear you're going on patrol. Where would you like your remains sent?" Carole grinned.

"I intend to survive the experience," Christine said. "Is sleeping behind the ShopMart required? If so, I'll bring a pillow and a blanket."

"Oh, no, you're not going to have time to take a nappy-poo," Carole grinned. "You're assigned to the best there is, the best there ever was, and the best there ever will be."

"Bret Hart?" Christine smiled.

"You should be so lucky. Connor is an Irish name, isn't it?"

"Yes, it is. What does that have to do with the price of peanuts?"

"You'll find out," Carole nodded. "And it's illegal to sell your penis in Stratford. Tell her, Vito."

"Hey, daydream believer; my sausage ain't for sale. Only Marie gets the big wazoo."

"This is going to be a lot more fun that I expected," Christine smiled. "This awful looking costume doesn't appear to be my size. Do you have a tailor here?"

"Sure," Carole smiled. "He works at the Town Dump; his name is Jimmy the Drunk. He buries corpses for us. Would you like to meet him?"

"Well, I might have a glass of fine Pinot Noir while he adjusts this outfit to fit my slender body. Where did you find a uniform to fit your lumpy physique? Pigs R Us?"

"I don't wear one. I'm the Commish. Sort of like your position, but add love and compassion for the common folk."

"A useless emotion born of a desperate attempt to be accepted by those below you," Christine smiled. "I suffer from no such delusion. Unlike yourself, I have had to evaluate many of the so-called common folk before hiring them. Most of them would remove the teeth from your mouth at night with a pair of pliers just to get the gold fillings."

"You keep thinking that way. You're doing a week here; if you try to back out, you'll spend the rest of that week in our holding cells. Do you like chuck steak with mashed potatoes, or Beefaroni? Your choice."

"Neither; I intend to order out if you incarcerate me, you little hedgehog."

"You won't be able to," Carole grinned. "Better have another pizza slice; it might be the only food you see for twenty four hours."

"What?" Christine exclaimed. "I require balanced nutrition."

"Fine; bring a little scale so you can see which Quarter Pounder weighs more than the other."

"I would never lower myself to eat that garbage," Christine snapped.

"You're going to be lowered a lot more than you expected," Carole said. "In body, mind, and spirit. You will be a different person at the end of the upcoming week. Last chance, Little Miss Broadway; you want out?"

"No, I do not. I took Harpie's challenge; I honor my word."

Stratford Police Department

900 Longbrook Ave.

Northern Patrol

Stratford, Connecticut

June, 2008

"Do you like my uniform?" Christine smiled as she twirled for Margo. "It was altered just for me."

"Aye, Lassie, I'll make sure they bury you in it," Detective Captain Margo Wilder-Williams smiled. "Get in me cruiser and shut yer yap."

"That's rather inhospitable of you," Christine smiled as she got into the car.

"You think that's bad? The day ain't over yet," Margo smiled. "I ain't known for me jovial personality. Why are you doin' this stupid shit? You ain't qualified to be no copper."

"It was a challenge issued by Harper."

"Oh, and you were stupid enough to take it? You got brain damage, girly? You know what you got yourself into?"

"Just police work," Christine shrugged. "Drive around in a car and hand out the occasional speeding ticket."

"Oh," Margo smiled. "Is that so? You believe what you want."

"And why is a Captain doing road duty?"

"Because I am a copper," Margo smiled. "I do me duty no matter what rank I wear. I like the road. Soon I will be Chief of Detectives for the Department, thanks to you overchargin' Carla for land to put a new police department on. Going on the road puts me in touch with the good people, who I have sworn to protect. You wouldn't know anything about that now, would you? Only thing you ever swore to protect is your bank account."

"I am a businessperson. I do not owe anybody anything except the excellent product of my mind. What did your mind ever produce?"

"Dead people," Margo nodded as she pulled up in front of Sid Weinberg's computer store. "You are about to get a lesson in police work. Ya come with me, and keep your trap shut. Just stand there and try to look like a tough guy. I will handle Sid."

"Sid did security work for me; what has he ever done to deserve you?" Christine said.

"He ain't Irish," Margo grinned. "He's a no good bastard Jew son of a bitch who worships the almighty dollar. Just like you."

"No!" Sid Weinberg screeched when he saw Margo. "I didn't do anything wrong! What do you want?"

"You done plenty wrong, you Jew heathen son of a bitch," Margo snarled as she slammed her night stick on the counter. "Now you got to pay for your sins, Sidney, and I am the bill collector."

"I'm an honest businessman!" Sid whined.

"Oh, like the rest of your Jew buddies who lend money at forty percent interest," Margo smiled.

"That's legal!" Sid screeched. "I forget the statute. I think it's an Israeli law. Besides, I don't lend money. I always help the police. Why do you always come in here and threaten me?"

"Because I got the badge and the gun and you don't," Margo smiled. "I am a Captain, and I can lock your Jew ass up anytime I want, and there ain't shit you can do about it. Now if you got an ounce of sense left in that Hebrew brain you got, you will help us. Otherwise, you deal with Blondie," Margo grinned, nodding at Christine. "She's new on the job and fired a perfect score at the range. She don't like your kind, either."

"I remember her; she's hot," Sid grinned. "She's a shiksa."

"What did you call me?" Christine shouted, her hand going to her sidearm.

"Shiksa. It's a Jewish word for a girl who isn't Jewish. You aren't Jewish, are you?"

"You never mind what I am," Christine snapped. "The law is not based on religion."

"Tell that to her," Sid said, nodding at Margo.

"Yeah," Margo grinned. "You tell me that, Blondie. This son of a bitch is a heathen Jew bastard. He has to pay the price for that, and the Irish are here to make sure it happens."

"We have freedom of religion," Christine said. "You can't pursue Sid because of his religious beliefs."

"Oh, I can't?" Margo smiled. "The boy can help us, but he won't. That makes him a conspirator."

"I'll help!" Sid whined. "I always help you menopause crazed policewomen."

"Oh, ya do, do ya, Sidney?" Margo smiled. "Ya think I got the curse and it affects me judgment, do ya?"

"Well, it could," Sid grinned. "I could fight you in court."

"Or you could fight me behind the building," Margo nodded. "Which one would work out better?"

"Well, if you put it that way," Sid shrugged. "What do you want?"

"Information about Bartram Edwards," Margo said. "By authority of Carla. Care to argue the point, boy?"

"No," Sid squeaked. "But you don't know what you're getting yourselves into."

"We will see about that," Margo said. "You get me that information. All of it, too. The fella is a crook."

Stratford Police Department

Northern Patrol

Paradise Green

Stratford, Connecticut

June, 2008

"Here we go," Margo said as a Corvette sped past Ray's Gulf at 110 miles an hour. "There's the law abiding people of Stratford." She hit the light bar and pulled out in pursuit. She called dispatch. "Unit 2205 in pursuit of a speeder, headed up Paradise Green towards Huntington Road. Request backup and a road block."

"What?" Pat Kennedy Junior said. "You're interrupting my lunch, Margo."

"Fuck you and your lunch with it," Margo snapped. "You block them roads, or else it's on you when some innocent civilian gets killed."

"Roger," Kennedy said. "They are on the way. What are you doing tonight?" he said.

"Not you, dummy. I'm married."

"So I've heard," Kennedy smiled. "You should see the Irish Python and reconsider your position."

"Go fuck yourself," Margo snarled.

"That was uncalled for," Kennedy said as he called five units to the Northern Area.

"Now you will see what police work is about," Margo said as she pursued the Corvette up Huntington Road, light bar flashing. A boy leaned out the window of the Corvette and gave Margo the finger.

"There you go," Margo sighed. "This is the trash you got in this town. What you think about your high and mighty bankbook saving you now, huh, Lassie?" she grinned as she floored the accelerator.

"Stop," Christine whispered. "You're going to hit them."

"That's the main idea," Margo said. Seconds later, she crashed into the Corvette with the ram on the front of the cruiser. The Corvette skewed wildly to one side and crashed into a tree. It exploded into a million pieces; the frame flew off into the woods accompanied by pieces of the two occupants. The scene became very quiet as Margo stopped and blocked the road.

"There you are," she sighed. "Them that got no respect for the law die by the law. Go get the body bags out of the trunk and pick up what's left of these boys. Do it not, and I will put you in one of them bags meself. You want to be a copper? Go do your duty."

"I have to pick up dead bodies?" Christine exclaimed.

"If I say so, you do," Margo nodded. "I picked up my share. Now it's your turn. Get to it."

"But this is a crime scene," Christine said. "You have to investigate."

"See these?" Margo said, tapping her Captain's bars with her stick. "I say what gets investigated here, and I say them boys was in the wrong. End of the investigation. Now move it, girly. I don't want the neighbors to see this mess. There's a bowling bag in me trunk if you find a head," she grinned.

The paramedics arrived along with the Fire Department and five cruisers. Pat Kennedy Sr. waddled over. He unwrapped a hot dog, farted, and looked around. "Any survivors?" he smiled.

"You serious?" Margo grinned.

"Good. Less paperwork," Pat said. "Is that Chrissy Connor over there puking?" he smiled.

"Yes it is," Christine gagged. "And do not call me Chrissy."

"Since when are you a cop? Business fail?" Kennedy said as he unwrapped a second dog.

"No. Harper challenged me to do this and I accepted."

"Care to try Sergeant next? Walk a mile in my shit stained underwear," Kennedy smiled as he ripped a horrible fart. "Uh oh …. that one had lumps. I think I'll go back to the station. Looks like you have the situation well in hand, Margo; the perps are all dead. Excellent work."

"Why thank ya kindly," Margo said as she curtsied. Kennedy went back to his Kelly Green cruiser and left.

"You think this is funny?" Christine said. "Two people in their twenties are dead."

"And not a minute too soon," Margo said. "Ya turn bastards like that loose on society and eventually they will kill somebody who don't deserve to die. I seen enough of that on this road; gal and all her kids got T-boned by one of these assholes; killed 'em all deader than Hayman. You want to clean up some little kids next?"

"No," Christine said, looking away. "I couldn't take seeing that."

"Aye, I didn't like it meself. Better to look at that," she said, nodding at the body bags. "Them boys will never harm nobody in my town."

"Got all the pieces?" Paramedic Jack Richards smiled as he came over.

"Who cares," Margo said. "We got enough for identification; leave the rest. Crows got to eat too, ya know."

"I was thinking Duchess might like to have a Shepherd's Pie special this week," Jack grinned. Christine groaned and ran behind a tree to vomit again. "What's wrong with her?" Jack said.

"Business girl," Margo grinned. "Owns that fancy assed car company in Lordship. Took a bet with Harper, and here she is playing at bein' a copper."

"Could have given her desk duty," Jack said.

"Now Jackie; that wouldn't be no fun now, would it?"

"I suppose not," Jack sighed. "I'll log in what's left of these dudes with the Coroner. Are their genitals intact?" he grinned. "There are rumors about her."

"Thelma Bridewell? Them ain't no rumors, boy. She likes to rife 'em hard and cold."

"I'd like to ride that," Jack grinned, nodding at Christine.

"Better you take one off Bridewell's slab," Margo sighed. "That gal got ice water in her veins. Thinks she is all there is, she does."

"What the …… you can't be serious. I refuse to eat here," Christine said as Margo pulled into McDonald's and parked.

"Suits me," Margo shrugged. "You can fuckin' starve to death for all I care, ya uppity bitch." She got out of the cruiser; three young men immediately put their hands on the trunks of their cars and spread their legs. "Real funny," Margo nodded. "Wait until it's for real."

"Waste anybody today, Margo?" one of them called out.

"Not intentionally," Margo smiled. "You want to be first?"

"We're law abiding citizens," a second boy said.

"Sure you are, ya fuckin' pot head," Margo said as she came over. "Get back in that position."

"You don't have probable cause," the boy said.

"Oh, a fuckin' lawyer, are ya? I don't need no probable cause because you are an asshole and probably got a score on you. What's this?" she smiled as she pulled a sandwich baggie out of the boy's jacket.

"Oregano," he grinned.

"Oh; then let's see if it goes with drain water; you can make pasta." She dumped the "oregano" into a storm drain.

"Hey! You can't do that!" the boy yelled. "You know what that cost me?"

"Oregano is cheap," Margo smiled. "Care to change your mind about what was in that bag?"

"You ….. you're going to push us too far one day, and that'll be it for you."

Margo kneed the boy in the groin from behind, then slammed him face first into the trunk of his car. "I'm waitin', boy," she whispered into his ear as he threw up on himself. "Take your best shot."

"Leave him alone," another boy said as he came up behind Margo.

"Best think twice about what you want to do," Margo said. "Assault on a police officer is good for ten years. Not that you'll know, because I will kill you deader than Buddy Holly if you put one finger on me." She turned around and stared the boy in the eye. "Do it," Margo nodded. The boy waved her off and went back to his car.

"Come on, Killer," Margo said to Christine. "Lunch time. You assholes take off. You got two minutes before I call Patrol and lock all of your asses up." The boys jumped into their cars and left.

"How did you do that?" Christine said. "They were genuinely afraid of you."

"It's right here," Margo said, tapping her temple. "Your will against theirs. Them boys know me, and they know I mean business. If I say I will kill a boy if he touches me, that boy goes to a funeral parlor that day, and they know it. That is how you avoid the whole thing."

"Fear?" Christine said.

"Call it what you want. It don't need a definition; all it needs is to work."

They went inside, and two girls behind the counter yelled "Get the donuts ready!"

"You're a wise ass little street whore," Margo laughed at the first girl. "Your price go down any since you got the clap?"

"Shit no," the girl laughed. "They deserve whatever they get if they don't use protection."

Christine looked up at the menu. "What is this awful food?" she exclaimed.

"Hamburgers, mostly," Margo said. "Ever have one?"

"Yes, at a fine restaurant; good ground sirloin cooked on a charcoal grill with a nice slice of fresh tomato and some lettuce."

"Here you get a good ground cow's ass on a sesame seed bun with pickles, mustard, and ketchup. Have some Fries with it; kills the taste."

"I can't eat this food," Christine said. "It has no nutritional value."

"Who gives a flying fuck?" Margo laughed. "It tastes good. It got the basic food groups; grease, salt, and cholesterol. Have the Quarter Pounder with Cheese Meal; you'll live. If you get too sick, I'll take you over to Doc Wells and have him give you a lethal injection."

"Thank you for your concern. All right, I'll have one. And those chicken things. They look good."

"Don't go by the pictures on the menu," Margo grinned. "Them McNuggets is made from the seagulls that drop dead after they eat the leftovers folks throw in the parking lot."

"Do you have to say something awful about everything I order?" Christine said.

"Well, it is The Rainbow Room. You can't be too careful." A call came in on Margo's radio. "Margo," she sighed. "Yeah, she's here. You want her to do what? Okay, I'll bring her back after we eat. Yeah. Mickey D's. She don't like it." She turned to Christine. "You're going on a drug bust with Clodagh and Harper," she grinned. "You got life insurance?"

"What the hell is this?" Clodagh sighed. "Take this off," she said, and yanked Christine's police jacket off. "Go change into civvies. You have five minutes."

"What are civvies?" Christine said.

"Everyday clothes."

"Oh; do you prefer Anton Stanofsky or….."

"Jeans and a sweatshirt," Clodagh said. "If you don't own any, Miss Manners, you're the same size as me. Raid my locker. Move it. The window of opportunity closes in ten minutes."

"What …. never mind," Christine said. She appeared five minutes later in jeans and a Uconn sweatshirt. "This is demeaning," she said. "I never had to dress like this. Even when I worked on the Assembly Line, I had custom made work clothes."

"I'll be sure to tell the undertaker to dress you nicely," Clodagh said. "You have a gun?"

"No."

"You do now," Clodagh said. She took a Colt .45 out of her bag, checked it and loaded it, and stuffed it into Christine's waistband. "The safety is on. I chose this because Fuck Face says you own one."

"What did you call me?" Harper shrieked as she loaded the B.A.R.

"Hard of hearing as well as stupid looking?" Clodagh grinned. "You got grenades?"

"Of course," Harper snapped. "No girl leaves home without them. You take the Thompson."

"Gren …. You're going to get me killed," Christine nodded. "I don't know how to do this."

"You do what we tell you," Clodagh said. "Nothing else. Put this on under your sweatshirt," she said, handing Christine a bulletproof vest. "We are going into Hell," she nodded. "Just be ready. Oh, here's an M-16A1 for you."

Harper drove; they parked two blocks over and walked to the address. Two black men stopped them halfway there. "What you white bitches doing here?" one man said.

"We came to fuck your mother in the ass with a broomstick," Harper said, pointing the B.A.R. at the man. "Ever see one of these?"

"Whoa!" the man said. "That be Saving Private Ryan shit."

"Yeah, but it isn't Saving Private Buckwheat," Harper smiled. "Now step off bro, and lose your memory. Or your life," she shrugged. "Your choice. Doesn't matter to me." The two men scampered off.

"They ran," Christine giggled. "You scared them off. I can do that, too."

"Sure you can," Harper sighed. "What are you going to do; threaten to give them the wrong color leather seats in their new Orion?"

"Well, most people would be very upset if I did that," Christine said.

"Just stay behind us, and watch your rear. Anybody runs up to us, shoot them. This isn't a wedding party invitation. These assholes down here make their money selling drugs, and we are all that stands in their way."

"Will our cruiser still be there when we want to leave?" Christine said.

"Nope," Harper said. "There's a surprise in the car for them. Patrol will come get us if we're still alive."

"Alive?" Christine exclaimed. "I want to be alive."

"The shut the hell up and watch the landscape."

"It doesn't make any sense," Christine sighed. "These people live like animals. They don't have good jobs because they never learned anything of value, so they poison each other with narcotics; why?"

"Relieves the stress and pain of being totally worthless assholes," Clodagh said. "Look, Chrissy, it isn't our job to save these douche bags. It's our job to keep the disease where it is so it doesn't spread around town."

"You view these people as having no value; I can understand that," Christine said.

"You do?" Harper said. "What the hell do you know about poverty, Miss Billionaire? And don't give me your jive about going to work in Daddy's factory with a peanut butter sandwich, either. Do you think I like the idea of coming down here and raiding these assholes and maybe killing them? I do not."

"I do," Clodagh grinned. "I like killing assholes."

"Shut up," Harper sighed. "Maybe you would have liked it better if you were one of them, but no; the police department saved you. Think about that. Do your job, and have a little feeling for the people you chase."

"You're starting to sound like Carla," Clodagh said.

"There are worse things in life than sounding like Carla," Harper said. "There's the building. Second floor; we go in from the first floor. This is a major drug operation, and I mean major. Rebel Lee has been working on this for four months. They all go if they resist. Got it?"

"Got it," Clodagh said as she stuck a 20 round magazine into the Thompson.

"Two guards," Harper whispered as they crept through the bushes near the porch of the old house. "Get down." She pulled the pin on a grenade and tossed it onto the porch.

"Motherfucker!" a huge black man screamed. Those were his last words as the grenade went off.

"Move!" Harper yelled. She went through the front door and tossed another grenade; it blew two armed men into pieces. Two more men came running down from the second floor; Clodagh cut them in half with the Thompson.

"This works great," she grinned as she changed out the magazine.

The house went silent; Harper held up her hand. She pointed up towards the second floor where she knew more men would be. Stair raids were suicidal; the advancing party stood almost no chance of survival. Harper made several hand signals and tossed Clodagh two grenades. She held up three fingers; Clodagh nodded in assent.

"What about me?" Christine whispered.

"Stay here," Harper whispered back. "Take out anybody who comes in from the street. Watch the stairwell; base of fire."

Harper crawled over to the base of the stairs; she knew that whoever was up there was waiting for her. She grinned at Clodagh and stood up. She lobbed a grenade up and over the railing onto the second floor; it went off, tearing out a wall. Screams of pain followed; Harper got down and motioned for Clodagh to follow up. Clodagh pulled the pins on two grenades; she tossed the first over the rail and started up the stairs with the other. She got down as a terrific blast blew out another wall; she threw the second grenade through the opening and hugged the stairs.

Harper ran past her with the B.A.R and emptied a magazine into the room that had been revealed; Clodagh followed, spraying the room with the Thompson. A man staggered out of a closet, gun in hand; Christine, who had come up the stairs, fired the grenade launcher under the M-16A1; it blew the man into a cloud of soup. Harper pulled her Python and checked the room for more men. There were none.

"Jeez, what a mess," Clodaagh laughed. "Even Bob Vila couldn't fix this place."

"Find the dope," Harper commanded. Two minutes later, Clodagh waved her over to a closet.

"There's enough shit in here to get the whole state high for a year," she grinned. "We could retire on this." Harper pointed her Python at Clodagh's head. "Just kidding," Clodagh said.

They rigged thermite charges and went outside. They shooed all the neighbors away and called the Fire Department. Pat Kennedy Sr. arrived with four police cruisers and three fire engines, and looked at Harper.

"Is this carnage necessary?" he smiled as he farted and unwrapped a hot dog.

"Could be," Harper grinned. "Stay away from our cruiser two blocks over."

"Gee, I wonder why," Kennedy said.

"Stay back. Just make sure the fire doesn't spread," Harper said to Fire Department Lieutenant Ralph Bosworth.

"I'd like to see you spread," Bosworth smiled as he directed his men. "I always had a thing for young boys."

"I bet you did," Harper said. "Your brother is living proof of that."

"He asked for it," Bosworth huffed. "It's a family tradition."

Just then, a tremendous roar sounded two blocks away. "That would be our cruiser," Harper grinned. "The local crooks must have tried to steal it."

"And sorry I bet they are for doing so," Kennedy smiled as he farted again. "If my services aren't needed here, Duchess has a special on Chili Dogs."

"We'll go with you; there isn't any evidence here worthy of an investigation, and I'm hungry. And we need a ride."

"I'll give you a ride, sonny boy," Bosworth smiled.

"Let's go," Harper said, pointing her Python at the front of Bosworth's pants. "Ride this."

"Uh, no thanks," Bosworth smiled.

"Surprise, surprise," Kennedy smiled as he pointed at his cruiser. "The Shamrockmobile awaits thee. Hot Dog Heaven is our next stop."

Duchess Diner

1000 Stratford Ave.

Stratford, Connecticut

June, 2008

"Oh, it's Kennedy," Janet smirked as everybody came in. "I guess we have to put on a second shift."

"My patronage here is legendary," Kennedy smiled. "Look at these fine young girls; they will follow in my footsteps."

"As long as they don't have to follow in your underwear," Janet said. "Where no man has gone before."

"I've gone in my underwear many times; I have the stains to prove it. Would you like to see?"

"No thanks," Janet smiled. "I was married twice; that was enough. I had to take this job to pay for all the Clorox. What is it with you guys, anyway? Didn't you ever hear of toilet paper?"

"By then it's too late," Kennedy smiled. "There is a police term for that; Paperus Poopus Interruptus. I'll have six hot dogs with the works, and six Jalapeno Chili Dogs with Chinese hot sauce."

"Planet Killers," Janet whispered. "Give me ten minutes to evacuate the building."

"As you wish, oh great douche bag of Stratford. Why did you get divorced, anyway? Was it your charming personality or your devastating good looks?"

"My hot pussy was too much for them," Janet grinned. "You want to see why?"

"No, I've had my share of investigating toxic waste dumps here in town. Raybestos polluted half the town; I'm sure what you have between your legs runs a close second. Or it just runs," Kennedy smiled.

"Extra mustard on those dogs coming right up," Janet cackled. "And that's the only hot dog a fat Irishman ever had that came right up. What do you girls want?"

"As many hot dogs as they can make," Harper said.

"Cheeseburger platters until I puke," Clodagh grinned.

"And Miss Fancy Pants?" Janet said, eyeing Christine.

"A medium rare burger cooked on a charcoal grill with French Fries and a sensible salad. Oh, and a fine Merlot," Christine said.

"Cheeseburger Platter with Ripple, cole slaw on the side," Janet grinned. "You got it."

"What's Ripple?" Christine said after Janet left.

"It's the best wine," Harper gushed. "You'll love it. All the finest people in Stratford drink it."

"Do you have a gas mask?" Clodagh said.

"No; Carole didn't issue me one; why?" Christine said.

"You'll find out after Kennedy eats those Planet Killers," Clodagh said.

"Good job," Carole said as she looked at the report. "It should only take about a year to fix all the damage you did on Stratford Avenue, and you only killed eleven people and a police cruiser. You must be slipping."

"We could go back and finish off the rest of the neighborhood," Harper grinned.

"Did you find the dope?" Carole said.

"Right there," Clodagh said, pointing at Harper.

"We burned it all with thermite," Harper said. "You leave that much stuff in the evidence room and people will be tunneling through the wall to get at it."

"Where's Christine? Sid called. He has some information for her and Margo."

"She had to go see Doc Wells," Harper said. "Kennedy ate six Planet Killers at Duchess, and she rode back here with him in his cruiser."

"That'll teach her to be a cop," Carole said. "So, what's next? Did you solve the Kennedy Assassination?"

"What a shame it must be to be an old person," Harper sighed. "No clue, no knowledge of our case load, and no clue what has already been done. Carla solved the Kennedy case. Where were you?"

"I was here," Carole shrugged. "I have a lot on my mind. Sometimes I forget things. Where is Carla, anyway?"

"She's on a leave of absence," Harper grinned. "Like your brain. Maybe you should invite Brian Wilson back here. He's in Bermuda this week."

"He is?" Carole exclaimed. "I'd like to go see him."

"Too bad. They won't let you into Bermuda, because you don't own any shorts," Harper said.

"Very funny. Go see Sid, and keep me informed."

"About what?" Clodagh said.

"I don't know," Carole said as she opened a pizza. "Whatever it is you're being paid to do that you don't do when I want you to."

"What do you want us to do?" Clodagh said.

"Protect and serve," Carole said as she shoved two pizza slices into her mouth. "Make Stratford a safe place for the people who live here."

"You'll be okay," Harper smiled. "Take a Tylenol and have a nap."

"This town is fucked," Clodagh nodded. "Just sit there and let us fix it."

Residence of Flannery Quinn

Old Farm Road

Bozeman, Montana

July, 2008

"Interesting," Flannery said as she looked over the information Harper had sent her. "This implicates Bartram Edwards in a monumental drug scheme. Where did this information come from?"

"Sid Weinberg, the computer dude who lives here in town. He used to be CIA. He still is, although he hasn't been used in a while. His information is reliable." Harper said.

"We have to have this independently verified," Flannery said. "Then we will act accordingly."

"I don't play the accordion. What do you need?" Harper said.

"Besides a lobotomy for you, we need flight records out of Mena Airport in Arkansas, where most of these drug shipments allegedly arrive. Then we need confirmation of these bank records attached to Edwards. That means grabbing up a high level person who we can convince to tell the truth. That's your job."

"I can do that," Harper said. "That's the easy part."

"People involved in a scheme this big won't give it up."

"Yes they will," Harper said. "Count on it. We've never failed. Doesn't matter who it is; Edwards, anybody you care to mention. What's next after we make our case?" The line went dead in Harper's hand. "Oh, that," she sighed. "I thought that's what you'd say."

Bubba's Adult Emporium

Barnum Avenue

Stratford, Connecticut

July, 2008

"Hi, I'm Bill Clinton," Bubba grinned. "I know you gals."

"How are you doing, Bill?" Harper smiled as she set two huge Burger King bags on the counter. "We need some help."

"Gals always need help," Bill rasped. "You want to see why I need help?" He pointed at the black curtain covering a portrait of Hillary and his daughter.

"No thanks, I've seen that before. This involves a drug scheme."

"I do not do drugs," Bill nodded, eyeing the Burger King bags. "My major failing is a Triple Double Bacon Cheese Whopper."

"There are ten of them in these bags," Harper grinned. "With Fries. Talk to me."

Bill eyed the bags. "What do you need?" he said.

"Bartram Edwards," Harper said. "I want to pop him for dealing drugs."

"No," Bill said, backing up. "You cannot do that. Are you insane?"

"Opinions vary," Harper said. "What's so special about him?"

"He has connections you cannot imagine," Bill said. "Best you leave this one alone."

"No, I will not," Harper said. "We have information that says he runs the biggest drug importation business in the country. That means he goes down, by any means necessary."

"You are gonna get this young kid killed," Bill said, nodding at Clodagh, who was looking through a pile of sex movies in the bargain bin. "That ain't right."

"Who the hell do you think you are, telling her I'm going to get killed?" Clodagh said. "I'll take these three," she said, tossing some videos onto the counter.

"You are underage," Bill said. "I cannot sell you anything of a sexual nature."

"Figures," Clodagh sighed. "Anything that's fun is usually illegal. Explain the fat girl you porked in the mouth in the White House."

"That was a consensual relationship," Bill said. "She was of legal age."

"Oh; that makes it all right," Clodagh said. "Stupid bastard," she smirked. "You lost your law license and almost got thrown out of office for a blowjob. Was it worth it? Why didn't you just admit to it? The whole thing would have …. blown over in a week."

"That's enough," Harper said. "Bill always helps us because despite his licentious ways, he is a patriot. Isn't that right, Bill?"

"I am," Bill nodded. "I did pull my pants down a time or two and I lied about it, but I love my country. Most men in the country do what I did."

"Most men in the country aren't the President," Clodagh smiled. "Make us a believer."

"Okay," Bill sighed. "There is a man who logs in all the flights coming into Mena, except for the ones from Afghanistan. He puts them in a separate log. That log is secret. He gets a piece of the action. His name is Gino De Marco. He got connections, if you know what I mean. He also got connections to Bart Edwards."

"What kind?" Harper said.

"You know," Bill shrugged. "Who do you think controls the drug business in this country?"

"You tell me," Harper said. "I can't wait."

"Giuseppe "Big Joe" Andolini. No relation to the Godfather movie. Not that anybody can prove," Bill grinned.

"Okay," Harper said. "Where does Big Joe live?"

"You are pushing me beyond my limit," Bill nodded. "I can only go so far."

"You can go into the ground, you bastard," Harper said, pulling her Python. "And it won't bother me one bit to put you there. Talk, motherfucker."

"St. Louis Missouri," Bill said. "East 77th Street. But you didn't hear that from me."

"Of course not," Harper said, holstering her Python. "It's always a pleasure to do business with the former President who now owns a porno shop."

"Man got to earn," Bill grinned. "That government pension ain't what it's cracked up to be."

"Neither are you," Harper snapped. "It's been nice forcing you to do the right thing. Maybe some day you'll figure out why we do the job we do for shit money ."

"Bye, Bill," Clodagh said as she grabbed the sex videos. "Don't like it? Call the cops."

Mena International Airport

Mena, Arkansas

Office of Gino De Marco

July, 2008

"Hello, Gino," Harper smiled as she walked into Gino's Office. "United States Assistant District Attorney Harper Cochran. This is Detective Clodagh McGuire from Stratford, Connecticut. We have a few questions for you."

"You can talk to the Airport Attorney," De Marco smiled. "He handles all our legal matters. I'm sure you understand."

"Oh, I do," Harper said. "You still have to answer my questions. You can have an attorney present. You have about five minutes to get one in here."

De Marco picked up the phone. "Send Attorney Sorrentino in here at once." He sat back in his chair.

Biagio Sorrentino came in; he looked at Harper. "What is this about?" he said.

"We have information that your pal DeNarco I mean DeMarco has been helping somebody run a major drug operation out of this airport," Harper said.

"That is ridiculous," Sorrentino said. "What is the basis for this charge?"

"Just a hunch," Harper said. "If he's so innocent, he can clear himself right now. Otherwise, off to jail he goes."

"What is your evidence?"

"Confidential," Harper said. "Revealing our evidence would only serve to alert other suspects who would flee the jurisdiction."

"So, you expect to waltz in here and question Mr. DeMarco over some allegation you made up? What law school did you flunk out of?"

"I didn't make it up, and I don't waltz. We prefer the Polka," Harper said. "DeMarco can either fess up and cooperate, or spend the rest of his life playing hide the salami in prison. I am also an FBI Agent and an Assistant Chief of Detectives. I can waltz, as you put it, into G.W.'s office any time I want, and get anything I want. Care to roll the dice with me? Oh, and I'm a professional wrestler, so I can beat the shit out of you if I feel like it."

"I see," Sorrentino said. "I think you are prejudiced against Italians."

"Who fucking cares what you think," Harper snapped. "And I couldn't care less if he's Italian. Either he talks or I take him out of here in handcuffs as an uncooperative material witness, and he can forget about life as he knows it."

"Give me a minute with Mr. DeMarco." Sorrentino took DeMarco aside, and they whispered back and forth. They then returned to DeMarco's desk. "Assuming there is some merit to your case, which we are not admitting, and assuming Mr. DeMarco knows anything of interest, what's in it for him if he cooperates?"

"Depends on what he knows. He has two choices; either he goes to the joint and needs his asshole reconstructed after two weeks, or he gets whacked by the dude he's covering for. Not very good options, you ask me."

"Certainly there must be option three," Sorrentino said. "I'm sure you know what I am referring to."

"I think so," Harper shrugged. "The Witness Relocation Program. To qualify for that, he has to have some really good shit."

"I need it in writing."

"I don't have a pen," Harper smiled. "Don't trust me? We'll play lock him up and see how long he can hold his breath. He'll talk after a few days of having a giant black dick shoved down his throat."

Sorrentino nodded at DeMarco, who nodded back. "He'll talk, but not here."

"Then let's boogey on down the road to the FBI," Harper smiled. "They'll put him someplace where he'll be safe. I'll catch up to him in a day or two. Oh, and we want all these filing cabinets and we want to search his home."

"Do you have a warrant?" Sorrentino said.

"No, but I would assume he's cooperating. If not, I can parade him around on TV so the world knows he's a rat. Your choice."

"Take whatever you want," DeMarco cried. "I knew this would happen some day."

"Yeah, but you did it anyway, didn't you, asshole," Clodagh smirked. "Does money mean that much to you?"

"It did," DeMarco said. "And when you deal with people like this you don't get any choices. They call it gold or lead. Play along and you'll be rich; otherwise, they kill you and make the offer to the next guy."

"You could have …. never mind," Harper sighed. "I'm tired of telling people like you what you could have done. Do you know how many bribes I could have taken in my ten years on the job? Good ones, too; from high level people. You know how many I took? None, because I couldn't live with myself if I did. I guess that's the difference between you and me. Stand up; you're under arrest."

"And don't take any sudden vacations, shyster," Clodagh said to Sorrentino. "You better come up clean yourself, or you'll be yodeling on some inmate's meat puppet."

"There is a U-Haul truck in my driveway," Flannery said as she looked outside; Debbie had a gun to the driver's head. "He said you sent this truck here. Is that true?"

"Yes," Harper said. "It's all the information about the ….. thing we talked about. I'm going to send you some help to decipher it. There is quite a bit."

"Okay, but you could have warned me. I don't like strange trucks pulling up to the house."

"Your number was busy," Harper said. "Black dude driving the truck?"

"Yes."

"Don't shoot the poor bastard; he's legit."

"They make good target practice," Flannery grinned. She hung up and went outside. "Driver's license," she said to the terrified driver. He handed it over. "Okay, Leroy, now we know who you are," Flannery said, trying not to laugh. "If this turns out to be a setup, you go first. Understand?"

"It ain't no setup!" Leroy squeaked. "Damn FBI sent me."

"You could be a faker," Flannery said, winking at Debbie. "What do you say, Debbie?"

"I say waste the son of a bitch," Debbie nodded. "Why take chances?"

"Hear that, Leroy?" Flannery said. "Your bitches are going to miss you," she grinned. "Is it true what they say about black men?" she smiled.

"Yeah," Leroy grinned. "We be like Arby's. We have the meats."

"Not that; I meant the fact that there are more of you in jail than in a Denzel Washington movie."

"Denzel be an honest man," Leroy nodded. "Me too."

"Okay," Flannery sighed. "You can go now. No tricks, either."

"Yes Ma'am," Leroy squeaked. "You gots it. I be on my way." Leroy jumped into the truck and tore down the driveway.

"Was that necessary?" Debbie sighed.

"No, but it was fun," Flannery grinned. "We don't get many visitors. Might as well take advantage of the ones we get."

"You really are diabolical," Debbie said.

"It's a gift. Let's see what's in the truck. You open the door."

"You better not hurt me," Sid Weinberg cried when he saw Margo. A wet stain spread across the front of his pants. "I did what you wanted."

"Ah, Sidney," Margo sighed as Commissioner Tracy O'Neil came in behind her. "Ya peed your britches. That ain't nice, doin' that in front of the police. We can lock you up for that."

"No!" Sid yelled. "I have a bladder condition."

"I see that; it's all over yer slacks," Tracy said as she opened a bag from O'Shaughnessy's Irish Deli. "See these?" she grinned, holding up a container of Trotters. "Pig's feet. You bastards don't fancy pork none, do you?"

"No," Sid squeaked as Tracy came closer. "Get those away from me. You can kill a Jew with pig's feet."

"I can kill ya with me Glock, too, ya stupid piece of shit," Tracy nodded. "I hear you been disrespectful to me cousin Margo here. Say yer sorry," she grinned.

"I'm sorry," Sid sobbed. "I would never do that. Margo is the most beautiful creature God ever made."

"Now yer talkin'," Margo nodded as she looked up. "Not like me milk bottle lookin' redhead cousin."

"Shit on you," Tracy snapped, "ya crippled up little bastard. Look at them legs you got compared to mine."

"Best thing about yer legs is they are wide open for business 24-7," Margo grinned.

"Can we get to why you're here?" Sid said. "I got that information about Bartram Edwards."

"Is the boy a crook?"

"That's up to you," Sid said. "He makes under two hundred grand a year as a Congressman. He has quite a bit of money in Nevis, Switzerland, and ….. Afghanistan."

"Uh oh," Tracy said. "That last one be a bit hard to handle. We are still at war over there. How much do the boy have?"

"Altogether, a hundred and ten billion."

"Wow, that would almost pay for an Irish birthday party," Tracy nodded. "What would a man want with that much money? Ya could never spend it all in a hundred lifetimes."

"It's a game," Sid said. "To see who can accumulate the most. Money is power. You have that much money, everybody is for sale."

"Not us," Tracy said. "And not nobody in our department. This boy is about to find that out the hard way."

Residence of Giuseppe "Big Joe" Andolini

East 77th Street

St. Louis, Missouri

July, 2008

"We'll never get in there," Harper sighed as she observed the office building through binoculars. "I've never seen security like this. It's supposed to be a residential address for the dude, not a fucking fortress."

"Nobody said it was a raised ranch," Clodagh said. "What did you expect? You think a zillionaire Mafia drug lord is going to live at the Honeyspot Motel in Stratford?"

"I wish he did," Harper said as she panned up and down the building. "Dimitri would give him up for a price."

"We can do this. We're cops," Clodagh said.

"It's a fucking office building sixteen stories high!" Harper exclaimed. "He has a suite on the top floor. The blueprints say elevators stop at fourteen. There is a helicopter pad on the roof. Look," she said, panning the roof. "Those are machine gun emplacements."

"Would Tom Hanks tuck tail and go home because somebody had some guns?"

"Tom is an actor, not a military tactician. Don't believe what you see in the movies."

"What's the mission?" Clodagh said. "Kill the son of a bitch, right?"

"Well, we do have enough information to corn-vict him," Harper grinned. "We just won't be able to get past all the guards. The first three floors of that building are not rented out. Guess what's going to be on those floors."

"Then we ignore the first three floors," Clodagh said. "This building is in the middle of ten unoccupied city blocks. There is no way to sneak up on it, and probably the Marines would have a hard time taking it down. Even if they did, Joey Big Nuts would be on that helicopter before they could get to him."

"Exactly. This requires some special tactics."

"Right. All we have to know is if he's in the building. Can we verify that?"

"I think so. We can set up surveillance on the helo pad. He'll show eventually."

"Can we make sure he shows up? Does he have any weaknesses?"

"Pussy," Harper grinned. "Word is he's worse than Bill Clinton ever dreamed of. What do you have in mind?"

"The Lovelace Triplets from the Honeyspot," Codagh grinned. "Who could resist an invite from them?"

"Anybody with a report from the Atlanta Disease Control Center," Harper sighed. "How the hell would we arrange that?"

"They have a website, and he has an address. They have videos of themselves on that site doing shit even Carla would turn down."

"Now there's something you don't see every day. Let's go home and talk to Dimitri."

The New Honeyspot Motel

Honeyspot Road

Stratford, Connecticut

July, 2008

"Hello, coppers," Dimitri Kolakov grinned when Harper and Clodagh came in. "Donuts are in the back."

"You're going to be in the back of our cruiser, you Commie son of a bitch," Harper said.

"I do nothing wrong. Dimitri is honest Russian businessman, same as Conrad Hilton. God bless Ronald Reagan."

"Is this dude for real?" Clodagh said. "Hey, Khrushchev; we need some help with a case. You'd better cooperate, or you'll be shoveling coal in Siberia for your pal Putin."

"Vladimir is great patriot," Dimitri huffed. "He loves Russia."

"But he isn't too fond of America. But let's forget politics; we need those tick infested whores you rent rooms to."

"You have the urge to merge?" Dimitri grinned. "These are nice Russian girls. They do not suck the biscuit."

"Not us, stupid," Clodagh said. "We need them to help us set up an international criminal."

"This criminal is not Russian, is he?" Dimitri said.

"Italian."

"Oh; in that case, Dimitri will help. What do you want Dimitri to do? Of course, there is something in it for Dimitri, right?"

"We'll waive prosecution for infecting half the state with these pigs you rent to," Harper smiled.

"These are nice Russian girls. The Lovelace Triplets are Avon Ladies."

"Sure they are. We want them to offer their …. services to a man in St. Louis. Can they do that?"

"Of course," Dimitri huffed. "They are famous world wide. Everybody wants to be with them."

"Only if they have a good urologist and life insurance," Harper sighed. "How are these three girls still alive?"

"Russian girl is tough," Dimitri said. "Like Russian man. Have natural immunity for cooties. Nothing bother these girls."

"If you say so. Here's the mark. You call us when they confirm the appointment. They don't have to go there, we just want this dude to think they're coming so he'll be home."

"Oh, Dimitri sees. This is setup for Carla to do assassination, right?"

"She's on vacation. You mind your own fucking business, pal, or you'll be first on her hit list when she gets back," Harper said.

Residence of Giuseppe "Big Joe" Andolini

East 77th Street

St. Louis, Missouri

July, 2008

"Hey boss, you got an offer," Dom Riggio said. "I think you should consider it."

"What's the offer?" Joe said.

"The Lovelace Triplets. They're some sort of International hookers. Even the Saudi Prince had them. You should think about it, you know what I'm saying?"

"How did they get my name?" Joe said.

"You know; that shit you post on line, on them sex sites. They don't know your real name or nothing; just your screen name; The Wonder Wanger."

"I like that name," Joe grinned. "You sure these dames is legit?"

"Yeah, they got a rep all over the planet. They'll do anything; they got videos. One of them screwed a donkey or something. We can screen them when they come in," Dom shrugged. "Nobody gets past security, if you know what I mean."

"Okay," Joe shrugged. "Set something up. How much?"

"Ten grand apiece."

"Marrone, they gotta be real good for that much dough. Do it," he grinned. "What do I have to lose."

"My God, not again," Cagney said when the Captain announced the presence of Carole, Harper, and Clodagh. "I should kill myself."

"I'll help," Carole said as she pushed the Captain out of the way and sat down.

"Careful," Cagney grinned. "That sofa isn't reinforced to hold that much weight."

"Screw you, Gary," Carole snapped.

"I told you about that," the Gary Busey lookalike said, pointing his pen at Carole. "I do not like being compared to that actor."

"You don't mind it when you sign his autograph for money," Carole grinned.

"That's different," Cagney said. "I can't help it if I look like him. Besides, I need the money."

"For what? Hooker night?" Carole said.

"That is none of your business. You try living in this place for thirty five years with no outside contact. I thought M.C. Hammer was something you buy at Home Depot. What do you want now?"

"Breakfast," Carole grinned. "Pancakes, bacon and eggs, and biscuits. And pizza."

"You know the number for the kitchen," Cagney smiled, handing her the phone. "I doubt there's a kitchen in the country whose number you don't know."

"Asshole," Carole muttered as she dialed. "You never did like me in high school."

"And I don't like you now," Cagney grinned. "There is no rational reason to let you into my facility."

"Yes there is," Carole said. "If you don't, I'll rat you out to Congress and tell them you violated your oath of secrecy. How many times have we been allowed to come in here?"

"Too many," Cagney grinned. "And this could be the final time. We have a lot of room in the desert for corpses."

"I made a video a long time ago," Carole smiled. "And I have pictures. Can you spell Leavenworth?"

"You'd actually blackmail me?" Cagney exclaimed.

"Sure; why not? That's what girls do when they don't get what they want."

"Nothing new there. What's this about?"

"Ask Harper. She'll fill you in on the details."

Ten minutes later, Cagney stared at Harper.

"Are you serious? I can't do that."

"You did it when we asked you to get rid of Kamatos," Harper smiled. "You even volunteered."

"That was different. He was an internationally known douche bag. Like Carole," Cagney grinned.

"Fact remains, you did it. This guy Andolini is the main man behind the biggest drug smuggling operation in the country. The dude who runs it is Bartram Edwards."

"What? Edwards? Are you insane? He's a Congressman!"

"And a drug dealer. I have his front man from Mena Airport locked up under protective custody. He is going to spill his guts in return for the Witness thingy. You should be in that," Harper snickered, "after all the whores you fucked out here. Isn't that illegal? Procuring prostitutes over state lines? I bet I could make that case …. stand up in court."

"That's about the only way you could make anything involving a man stand up," Cagney grinned. "Okay, I trust you, idiot that I am. What method do you want me to use?"

Harper leaned over and whispered into Cagney's ear.

"Jesus no," he sighed. "I can't do that."

"Yes you can, and you will," Harper said. "Because it's the right thing to do, and you know it. We can't get through the level of security this guy has without starting a major war. There is no other way."

"What about Edwards?" Cagney said.

"Ehhhhh," Harper shrugged, wiggling her fingers. "We'll take care of him. It is what it is; you know what I'm saying?"

"I should just shoot myself; I don't deserve this," Cagney sighed.

"Nobody deserves this," Harper sighed. "Women being forcibly hooked on drugs and being forced into prostitution to pay for the drugs. Carla and I have fought against this all our lives. Why won't you help us?" she said. "You are a good man; I know you are. Do something for once in your life to help the poor and innocent."

"Okay," Cagney said after a long pause. "You're on. My God, what did I ever do to deserve you people."

"You took an oath," Harper said as she stood up. "So did I. Try honoring yours; it extends beyond the military."

Residence of Giuseppe "Big Joe" Andolini

East 77th Street

St. Louis, Missouri

July, 2008

"Hey boss, the girls should be here in an hour. I got confirmation from the airline ticket broad. They land in twenty minutes, then a cab ride over here. We got our man Carmine at the cab stand to bring them over. Youse is home free."

"Okay; have Mario make some pasta and bread. Girls like to eat. We can drink some wine, eat, then do the badda-bing all night long."

"I'm way ahead of you, Boss. Mario is making Lasagna and Ziti with meatballs as we speak. Nobody cooks like Mario."

Office of the Base Commander

Major General Michael Wilding

Ramstein Air Base

Rhineland-Palatinate, Germany

July, 2008

"Yes, Miss Cochran, the General called. He said to give you whatever you want," Major General Wilding said.

"Oh, that would be nice, Big Mike," Harper gushed. "I hear you're very handsome. I'd like to see why they call you Big Mike."

"It's my I.Q., not my ….. you know. I remember you," Wilding said. "You work with Carla. You're the …. manly looking one."

"What did you say?" Harper shrieked. "I know where Germany is, you know; it's next to Pennsylvania. I'll come down there and lay an ass beating on you the likes of which you've never seen."

"You'll still look like a twelve year old boy after you do," Wilding grinned. "Let's get this done. I have two fast trackers from an aircraft carrier on the way to you. Can you confirm the target?" Wilding gave Harper the coordinates.

"Is that a zip code?" Harper said.

"No, it is not. Make it quick; F-15s fly fast."

"It's some Mafia asshole's building in St. Louis. Just take it out, okay?"

"All right," Wilding said. "I see it on the TV screen."

"Is I Love Lucy on?" Harper grinned. "I like that show. Loooooooo-cy! Ricky wants a blowjob."

"I hear he got more than his share, but not from her."

"Probably why they got divorced," Harper muttered. "I never did like that red lipstick she wore. I bet Ethel Mertz gave good head, though. I hear airplanes."

"Good. I suggest you take cover if you're near that building."

Residence of Giuseppe "Big Joe" Andolini

East 77th Street

St. Louis, Missouri

July, 2008

"What's that noise?" Big Joe said. "Sounds like military airplanes. They got no base around here."

Dom pulled the drapes open and stared in disbelief as the two F-15s came straight at them. "Get down!" he screamed.

The fighters discharged their missiles and banked away to the east. Joe ran for the safety of his bedroom.

"I guess we ain't getting laid tonight," Dom whispered as a missile tore through the wall and vaporized him. When the raid was over, there was nothing left of the building save a smoking hole in the ground.

"Let's go," Harper said to Clodagh. "Mission accomplished. Edwards is next after my asshole sister helps Flannery read what's in those filing cabinets."

"We could read what's in those filing cabinets," Clodagh grinned. "I could, anyway."

"Oh, I get it," Harper said. "You're suggesting that I'm stupid."

"You aren't as stupid as you look," Clodagh said. "Did you even look in those filing cabinets before you confiscated them?"

"Why should I? That's not my job. That is the job of my underlings," Harper said.

"You shit your underlings last week after drinking a twelve pack," Clodagh grinned.

"That was an accident!" Harper yelled. "Mary was in the bathroom; I had no choice."

"Okay, let's go get some food. Maybe we'll get to kill a waitress. We aren't known in St. Louis, are we?"

"No," Harper grinned. "I don't think so."

"Wendy, Wendy what went wrong; oh so wrong….. no hamburger should take so long, oh so long….. I never thought a guy could cry, til he caught his penis in his fly, oh Wendy; Wendy left me alone," Harper sang as the waitress waited, snapping way at her gum.

"You through?" the waitress said. "This ain't the audition for I Wish I Could Fucking Sing."

"And what are you auditioning for?" Clodagh smiled. "Gum whacking whore of the month? You should appreciate the Beach Bums music. You look old enough."

"You ain't that bright, are you," the waitress smiled. "I wasn't even born when them idiots started singing. You want food, or a good ass kicking?"

"Do I get to choose?" Clodagh grinned.

"Yeah," the waitress grinned. "We got five funeral parlors in town. Pick one."

"I see you like to negotiate," Clodagh said. "Maybe you should pick one."

"Okay," the waitress sighed. "I got to do this according to law, or I could get prosecuted after I kill you." She took out her martial arts card and showed it to Clodagh.

"Whoa," Clodagh said. "Master, Ninjutsu? Red Sash?"

"Hey, I got issues," the waitress shrugged. "You want some of me?"

"It isn't worth it," Clodagh said. "I know Krav maga. It was developed by the Israeli Defense Force."

"Yeah, that's cool," the waitress shrugged. "I killed a guy who knew that. You got a couple of flaws in that system. Want a private lesson?" she grinned.

"I think I'd rather have a cheeseburger platter," Clodagh smiled.

"Good choice," the waitress said as she wrote. "What about you, Mister?" she smiled at Harper.

"Oh my God," Clodagh giggled. "She's got your number."

"I'm a woman!" Harper shrieked. "I'm a professional wrestler, too. I could kick your ass; no marital artist can beat a wrestler."

"That's martial, not marital."

"Depends on how many marriage offers you've had," Harper huffed.

"I bet I know how many you've had," the waitress grinned, making a zero sign with her fingers.

"We're cops," Harper said. "So there. Now what do you have to say?"

"I say order something," the waitress said.

"I'll have what she's having," Harper said. "It better be good, too. Hey; do you have any people here we can kick the crap out of? It's a tradition."

"Bruce isn't busy," the waitress grinned. "He'll take you on, Miss Wrestler."

"Bruce?" Harper smiled, bending her wrist. "Wow, I'm afraid. Is he going to hit me with his purse?"

"Let's find out," the waitress smiled. She called for Bruce, who pranced over.

"What is it?" he lisped.

"The tough guy here wants to beat somebody up. I figure you're her type."

"This skank?" Bruce huffed. "Even RuPaul wouldn't go near her; she is much too manly. Do you wish to fight, sweetheart?" he smiled.

"This won't take long," Harper said as she got up. "Outside, Nancy."

Harper limped back in five minutes later, nursing a cut lip and a swollen eye.

"You got your ass kicked by a sissy," Clodagh giggled as Bruce sashayed back in and waved at them.

"Shut up," Harper snapped as she took ice from her water glass and put it in a napkin for her eye. "Bastard sucker punched me."

"Oh, and you let him? What the hell kind of wrestler are you? Never turn your back on an opponent. You don't know that dude; he could have been Bruce Lee in a skirt for all you know."

"Well, he didn't look very masculine," Harper grinned. "Everybody has to lose one occasionally," she sighed. "Let's eat and get back home."

"Hello," Tanner Lee smiled. "I'm Harper's sister. Can we get this over with? I don't like Montana. It's too hot here."

"Come back in the winter," Flannery said. "I believe the record is minus 59 degrees."

"Charming. It's ninety degrees outside. How do you explain that?"

"I don't," Flannery said. "Your job is to analyze the contents of these filing cabinets," Flannery said, pointing at the collection in the living room.

"That will take days," Tanner Lee said. "Where do I sleep?"

"In the barn," Flannery said.

"I refuse to bunk with animals," Tanner Lee said.

"You live with Harper and Carla," Flannery said. "You should be used to it."

"Point well taken. I demand good quality food and decent sleeping quarters."

"Sleeping bags are in the basement; go pick one. Debbie does the cooking. I'm sure you'll like her cuisine."

Debbie announced the evening meal at five sharp. Everyone sat down at the kitchen table. Debbie passed out military metal trays and silverware.

"What are these?" Tanner Lee exclaimed. "I'm used to fine China, and quality food cooked by the Negro Carla hired."

"Good for you," Debbie said. "Eat what I give you or starve to death." She produced a huge pot of mashed potatoes loaded with cheese and scooped three big helpings onto each tray. She then produced a big tray of meat from the oven's broiler; she tossed what resembled a big steak onto each tray.

"What's this?" Tanner Lee said, eyeing the steak. "It has a bone in it."

"Meat," Debbie grinned. "Don't ask what kind; they don't tell us that. If it's good enough for the Army, it's good enough for you." She then ladled a thick, greasy gravy and mixed vegetables over the potatoes, and shoved a huge wedge of Cherry pie into the mess. She then put a huge loaf of fresh baked bread on the table, along with a knife. "Now that's what I call dinner," Debbie nodded. "Just what a growing girl needs."

"This is crap," Tanner Lee said. "Our dog wouldn't eat this."

"Your dog ain't here," Debbie smirked. "You are. You eat what I give you, and be glad you got it. Otherwise, you can do your work on an empty stomach. Who the hell do you think you are, anyway? Some high and mighty debutante who expects caviar and Porterhouse steak every night?"

"That would be nice," Tanner Lee smiled. "It would be better than this garbage."

"Brave people who died for their country ate food like this," Debbie nodded. "So did we. You think you're better than them?"

"I do," Tanner Lee smirked. "I am superior to humans, even though I am one. I was raised by a superior species."

"Well lad-de-fucking-dah," Debbie smiled. "Tell you what, Miss Superior Species; you are in my world now, and you ain't shit here. I will train you, I will PT you until you piss blood, and I will make you wish you were never born. Do not fuck with me. Now shut the fuck up and eat your dinner; do it not, and you won't get another one."

"She can do it, too," Flannery smiled. "We were track stars in Catholic school. We can run your ass into the ground. This meal is designed to give you strength and the calories you need to withstand West Point training."

"This isn't West Point," Tanner Lee said.

"It is as far as you're concerned," Debbie grinned. "You are going to get a reality check, you uppity little bitch. We'll see how superior you are after a few days here. You might as well get used to it, because there is no way for you to escape from here. Now eat your dinner; training starts at five A.M."

"Get up!" Debbie yelled at five A.M. "Breakfast is in twenty minutes, after the morning run. Move it!"

"Morning run?" Tanner Lee exclaimed. "I can't run in the morning. I can't even run in the afternoon. I want to go home."

"Too fucking bad," Debbie snarled. She grabbed Tanner Lee by the hair and dragged her out of bed. "Get dressed. You have two minutes."

Tanner Lee appeared on the dirt road that was Flannery's driveway. "All the way down, and all the way back," Debbie grinned. "If you don't make it, you don't eat anymore."

"As if that would be some great punishment," Tanner Lee muttered. "I know things that can disable you," she smiled. "I'm tougher than you think I am."

"Then do it," Debbie said, shoving Tanner Lee hard in the chest. "Let's see what you've got, Space Angel."

"I cannot," Tanner Lee said. "I work for the police. I cannot hurt another human who is on our side."

"I can," Debbie grinned. "And you're it if you don't finish the morning run. Now move out, troop."

Ten minutes later, Tanner Lee collapsed in front of the house after completing the run. Debbie picked her up by the hair, dragged her inside, and threw her into a chair at the breakfast table.

"You may have some value after all," Debbie smiled as Flannery served breakfast. "A couple of weeks of this and you'll be a new person."

"I don't want to be a new person!" Tanner Lee exclaimed. "I want to be the old one."

"Yeah; lazy, useless, and conceited. Too bad for you, kid. You're stuck here. It's my way or the highway."

"This looks good," Tanner Lee said as she viewed the bacon and eggs cooked in lard, grits, home fries, toast, biscuits, pastry, orange juice, and coffee.

"Earn it," Flannery said as she sat down. "That is all we ask of you. That is all our country ever asked of us."

"I do not understand this country thing," Tanner Lee. "It is gang barbarism. Where I grew up, everyone is equal. We all had the betterment of the species in mind."

"Welcome to Earth," Flannery smiled. "We believe in that principle too, but most people who are in power do not. They seek to rule everyone by force. We will not be ruled by politicians."

"Then why do you let them assume power?" Tanner Lee said.

"That's our system. The people choose their leaders; most of the candidates are lying skunks, but how do you know until you elect them? You do not. After that, there is the endless quest to take back the power you gave them."

"In my world we do not have such a system," Tanner Lee shrugged. "The Supreme Council is made up of people who have ruled for thousands of years with only our best interest in mind. We do not have wars, criminals, or courts. There is no need for courts or elections."

"You never have somebody who goes nuts and takes things into their own hands?" Debbie said.

"Yes, occasionally. There was the case of Daniel 88779, about seven hundred years ago. He decided he would take over the Council by force. They ….. eliminated him," Tanner Lee grinned. "There have been no such incidents since. We are not a violent people as a rule, but we can be if it is necessary."

"We are," Flannery said. "I don't know why and I don't pretend to. It is what it is, and you deal with it. We have our own methods of getting rid of dishonest leaders."

"I can imagine what they are, based upon what blabby Carla says in her sleep. I've seen her methods being applied."

"Stick around and you'll see ours being applied," Flannery said. "You just don't get it, do you?"

"I understand what happens here as compared to where I was raised. That doesn't mean I approve of it."

"Then why are you here?" Debbie said. "Why didn't you stay on fucking Mars, or wherever the hell you came from?"

"You don't have to be insulting and use profanity," Tanner Lee said. "I am here because my sister brought me here. Perhaps if I had known what kind of place this was, I would have resisted."

"Too late now," Debbie said. "You're stuck here. Make the best of it."

"By doing what? Killing people?" Tanner Lee said.

"Nobody asked you to kill anybody," Debbie said. "There's your job," she said, pointing at the filing cabinets. "Make a case for us against Bartram Edwards. Then you can go back to Stratford, as if that's any bargain. Me, I like Montana. People here respect freedom. You screw around with people out here, all you get is dead."

"Are you going to kill this Edwards person?"

"That isn't up to us," Debbie said, "although with Harper running the show it is a distinct possibility."

"Then why do you have courts?" Tanner Lee said.

"Beats the shit out of me," Debbie said. "I like our system better. It has the same result, but it's faster and cheaper."

"Money," Tanner Lee sighed. "That's all humans here care about."

Residence of Flannery Quinn

Old Farm Road

Bozeman, Montana

August, 2008

"Here you are," Tanner Lee said as she set a manila folder on the table. "This is my report. The man is a no good crook and a drug dealer. This is your copy. The report contains references to the documents that prove the case, all of which are numbered. You have to ship the filing cabinets back to Connecticut under my seal."

"You shaped up well. Tan, lean, and mean. How do you feel?" Flannery said.

"Like a new person. Physically, that is. I could join the human Army and become a leader."

"Not a chance," Flannery said. "You don't have the right attitude. Debbie and I spent four years training military leaders; you don't have what it takes."

"Why not? I'm smart," Tanner Lee huffed.

"So were all the people we tossed out of the program," Flannery said. "There's an old saying; don't let your alligator mouth overrun your tadpole ass."

"What does that mean?"

"It means talking tough when you aren't just gets you and your troops killed. Tough isn't something you can fake; either you have it or you don't. You don't."

"I can be tough," Tanner Lee said.

"Okay; let's see just how tough you are," Flannery said. She put her .45 and a bayonet on the table. "Go outside with Debbie, and kill her. That's an order."

"What?" Tanner Lee laughed. "Why would I do that?"

"Because I ordered you to. In combat, you follow orders or you get shot by your own commanding officer. You don't get to make choices about what orders you follow."

"That is an illegal order," Tanner Lee said.

"There are no legalities on the battlefield; I didn't say why you should kill Debbie; that decision is mine. Maybe she's a spy or an insurgent; she is the enemy. The mission of the Army is to kill the enemy. Now get off your ass, and kill Debbie."

Tanner Lee looked at the .45 for a long minute. "I cannot," she sighed.

"I already knew that," Flannery said as she put the weapons away. "Don't get any funny ideas about joining the military. You aren't qualified."

"Well, I can accept that. I did my job here. I want transportation back home."

"Debbie will take you to the airport," Flannery said, standing up. She shook Tanner Lee's hand. "Thank you for your help," she said.

State of Connecticut Department of Criminal Justice

Office of the State's Attorney, Geographical Area No. 2

Office of D.A. Brenda DiCenzo

172 Golden Hill Street, Bridgeport, CT

August, 2008

"Whoa, you got a lot of good shit here," Brenda said. "I don't know if I can prosecute this dude, though. This is a federal beef. You gotta go see Donna I Don't Wanna."

"Who?" Tanner Lee said.

"Donna Melito. She's the U.S. Attorney for this District. Even then, this might have to be tried in the Washington Circuit because that's where the asshole lives."

"He has a summer home in Guilford," Tanner Lee smiled. "Nobody knows about it, because it's in his whore girlfriend's name."

"Carla?" Brenda said.

"No, not Carla," Tanner Lee said. "Do you think she'd be screwing a crooked Congressman?"

"It is what it is," Brenda shrugged. "She got like the urge, you know what I'm saying?"

"It isn't Carla. It's a dirty invader from Brazil."

"Oh, I see. Brazil? Them girls are gold digging pigs. They'll fuck your teeth out for a Taco. She got papers?"

"Other than the No-Pest Strip in her panties? She is here on a tourist Visa."

"I bet it's expired, too," Brenda grinned. "You got info on her?"

"I'm working on it," Tanner Lee said. "What about all this work I did? You can't prosecute him here?"

"You got to prove he did some of this corruption while he was in Connecticut. Then I can rack him up and get a federal indictment for the Washington Circuit through Donna. I got to have something where he like broke state laws. You get that for me, and I'll have him picked up pronto."

"Okay, I'll go to Guilford and investigate. Where the hell is Guilford?"

"Interstate 95 North; starts around exit 59. Nice town full of rich assholes who got boats and shit. This broad ain't gonna answer the door, you know."

"Then how do I ….. never mind. I'm sure Harper and Jackie will know how to interrogate her."

"I like didn't hear that," Brenda said, holding up her hands as a delivery boy from Collici's Italian Pavilion came in. "You want pizza?"

"I'm watching my weight," Tanner Lee smiled.

"Yeah, me too," Brenda said as she shoveled four slices onto a plate. "Cheers."

Stratford Police Department

900 Longbrook Ave.

Stratford, Connecticut

August, 2008

"Look at her," Detective Jackie Jasper giggled as Harper snored away at her desk, mumbling something in her sleep about Spanish dudes as she stuck her hand down the front of her pants. "Get the camcorder."

"Why?" Tanner Lee said.

"Blackmail value. We can get a raise out of this, and a promotion."

"That's dishonest," Tanner Lee said.

"You think?" Jackie said. "How do you think you get ahead in this world?"

"She likes to burn people at the stake," Tanner Lee whispered.

"Who cares," Jackie said. "I watched one of those stake burnings. I have pictures. She'll fold. You wanna be a Lieutenant some day?"

"I cannot extort Harper. You do it," Tanner Lee grinned.

Jackie walked over and kicked Harper off her chair onto the floor. "Hey! Daydream Beaver Believer! Wake the fuck up, asshole! And who the hell is Marco?"

"I was on my break," Harper muttered as she slowly got up. "I don't know anybody named Marco."

"Oh no, you were just mumbling his name for the last five minutes," Jackie smiled as she held up the camcorder. "We got it on tape."

"I only have forty dollars," Harper said quickly. "You can't shake me down. What do you want?"

"Numb Nuts here found a way to have Brenda prosecute Edwards in Connecticut. We have to go to Guilford and check out his main squeeze; some Brazilian douche bag. He paid for a beach house and put it in her name. We have to prove that, and that he used illegal funds to do it. That's what Brenda wants."

"Fucking Brazilians," Harper muttered as she fixed her pants. "Why is it always a Brazilian? Why not a hot Scotty who looks like Audrey Hepburn? I deserve to be a kept woman."

"Kept where? In a dog house?" Jackie laughed. "Come on, stick girl; look in the mirror. Brazilian girls have boobs, unlike you. And several other body parts you are sadly lacking."

"Up yours," Harper snapped. "I know where Guilford is; Carla and I went through it at 140 miles an hour a few times. I know how to get information out of town officials and bankers."

"Just don't wear a skirt," Jackie grinned. "You'll confuse them as to your gender."

"What's good for the goose is good for the gender," Harper said. "Let's go."

"Police," Harper said, holding up her badge.

"That's an Oreo cookie," Art smiled.

"Oh. I was on my lunch break. Here," she said, holding up her badge.

"That's from Stratford," Art said.

"So are we," Harper said. "We need information."

"What kind? The location of the local donut shop?" Art grinned.

"Oh, you're a funny one, aren't you," Harper said. "I'm Chief Harper Cochran. Ever hear of me?"

"Nope. You are free to look at public records," Art sighed. "Anything else requires a subpoena."

"We want to look at the public records for a beach house in the name of a Brazilian douche bag," Harper said.

"Address, please," Art said.

"I knew you'd ask that," Harper said. "We don't have that. It's a secret."

"Name of the ….. douche bag?" Art said.

"We don't have that either. You should be able to find it for us."

"How?"

"They are all named Maria Del something. Come on, Artie; cooperate and we'll burn the video of you screwing that goat at the Guilford Farm."

"There is no Guilford Farm, and I do not screw animals. That would include you," he grinned. "What are you, by the way? A rather ungainly version of the Rhesus Monkey?"

"What?" Harper shrieked. "I'm hot. And Reese's makes peanut butter cups, not monkeys. Now how about a little cooperation?"

"And if I refuse?" Art said. Harper took out her Python. "I see. I'll have a look," Art said. Five minutes later, he printed out a file. "Here you go; Maria Pereira. 150 Little Harbor Road. Last house on the street. Only person in town with a Portuguese name. No mortgage, no liens."

Town of Guilford

150 Little Harbor Road

Guilford, Connecticut

August, 2008

"There it is," Harper said as she pulled over a block away from the house. A young woman was sunning herself in a chaise lounge on the beach, squirting oil all over her voluptuous body. "Look at that," she said. "That is truly disgusting, doing that in public."

"It's private property," Jackie said. "She can oil her tits all she wants. At least she has some," she grinned.

"Fuck you. I have a nice pair of 34s. Can we arrest her for that?"

"No, we cannot. We have to prove Edwards paid for the place, dummy."

"Okay; there is no mortgage. What do we do about that?"

"Look up the realtor who sold the house," Tanner Lee sighed. "Are you really that stupid, or did you take lessons?"

"It's a natural talent," Harper said. "Look it up on your phone."

"Lourdes Silva," Tanner Lee said a minute later. "Another Brazilian."

"Now you're talking," Harper said. "We'll squeeze her for the information about the closing attorney."

"Good idea, asshole," Tanner Lee giggled.

Half an hour later, they had the name of the attorney.

Office of Attorney Carlito Santos

225 Main Street

Guilford, Connecticut

August, 2008

"Police," Harper said as she pushed her way past an irate secretary and marched into Carlito's office. "Call off your dog, or I'll put her on life support."

Carlito waved off the secretary, who gave Harper the finger and went back to her desk. "What do you want?"

"Information about a closing you did," Harper said.

"Do you have a warrant or a subpoena?" Carlito said.

"Yeah, we do," Harper grinned. "Show it to him, Jackie."

Jackie went behind Carlito's desk and grabbed him in a rear naked choke hold. She put him down on the floor and whispered into his ear. "Cooperate, Paco, or I'll snap your fucking neck."

"Okay! Let go!" Carlito said. "Jesus, you could have asked."

"We did," Harper said as she grabbed a canister of red licorice off Carlito's desk. "You resisted and asked for a warrant. That is very bad for you."

"What is this about?" Carlito said.

"Maria Pereira. You did a closing for her. Details, please," Harper smiled as she chewed away at the licorice.

"I don't remember that name," Carlito said.

"Oh," Jackie said. "He doesn't remember the name. It was only two years ago, dude. You have brain damage or amnesia? That choke hold can be reapplied, and I guarantee it will improve your memory."

"Let me look for the file," Carlito said. He dug through a filing cabinet and produced the file. "Here."

"Where did the funds to pay for this house come from?" Harper said.

"Maria brought the money to the closing," Carlito said.

"In what form?"

"Cash."

"Oh, okay. So a thirty year old Brazilian on an expired tourist Visa sashays in here with four hundred grand in cash, and you don't ask any questions?" Harper said.

"I don't have to," Carlito said. "That is not my job."

"Oh, but it is," Harper grinned. "You have to file paperwork with the feds for a transaction that large. You didn't do it, did you?"

"No," Carlito said, looking away. "There are some things you don't do if you want to stay alive."

"We don't care if you stay alive," Harper smiled. "That's what you don't understand. Name, please. Who gave her the cash?"

"I don't know," Carlito said.

"Okay; kiss your law license and your life good-bye," Harper said. "I'll make sure your stupid fucking face is splashed all over the interweb and all the news channels as a rat, and the dude who gave Maria that cash will see it. You won't live twenty four hours."

"No! You can't do that to me!" Carlito exclaimed.

"Sure I can, and I will," Harper said. "You see, Carlito, we don't like crooks. We lock them up, and you're next unless you come clean."

"They'll kill me," Carlito sighed as he slumped into his chair. "I'm the only one who knows about this, and ….. the person knows that. You are giving me a death sentence."

"You gave it to yourself, you no good bastard," Jackie smiled. "You did this; reap it, motherfucker."

"You'd let me die over a real estate transaction?" Carlito exclaimed.

"Like that," Harper said, snapping her fingers. "Won't be the first time, or the last. Who the fuck needs you?" she laughed. "Talk or die; your choice. I'll see if I can get you in to the WRP. Deal expires in three seconds. Three, two…."

"I'll take the deal," Carlito said. "My wife will kill me for this."

"Luck of the draw," Harper said. "Maybe she should have married an honest person."

On the way out, Harper went over to Carlito's secretary. "You gave me the bird, you no good Spic bitch," she smiled. "I don't like that."

"Who cares what you like, pig," the girl grinned. "Go fuck yourself."

"She told me to go fuck myself," Harper laughed. "I think I'd rather fuck you, whore." She grabbed the girl by the hair and slammed her into a wall. She then opened the girl's top desk drawer and stuck her head into it, then slammed the drawer closed three times as hard as she could. She then threw the girl out the window without opening it. "Whoa, that will leave a mark," she said as the girl thrashed around on the sidewalk below. "Welcome to America!" she yelled at the girl.

Office of the United States Attorney Donna J Melito

Eastern District of Connecticut at Bridgeport

Lafayette Boulevard, Bridgeport, CT

August, 2008

"This is cool," Donna said as she spritzed herself with Chanel. "I can like do this."

"You have to read the file," Harper smiled

"I like read it," Donna said. "It's cool."

"Cool," Harper sighed. "Is that a legal term?"

"Yeah, it is," Donna said. "You got a problem with the way I do my job? We could like go outside and settle that."

"No," Harper said. "I don't have a problem with you, other than the fact that you graduated with Carole, which makes you old enough to be my grandmother. I bet you play the Beach Bums," she grinned.

"Yeah, I do. Brian Wilson is like a legend."

"Brian is like retarded," Harper said. "Old People's music. You are old people."

"So? You think you know more than me because I'm older than you? I killed more suspects, made more busts, and locked up more drug dealing pricks than you ever did. You got an affidavit from this dude Carlito? You need that to make a case."

"Right here," Harper said, handing over the affidavit.

"This is notarized by Tanner Lee," Donna said. "Hardly an independent person."

"She's honest," Harper said.

"You think Canfield will say that? He'll take this case because he hates you, and you got a real high burden of proof here. An affidavit signed by your sister doesn't cut it. You say this whore showed up at the closing with a bag of cash? Prove it, with more than an affidavit from a dude who fears for his life. You get me that independent proof and we will move forward."

"Okay," Harper shrugged.

"I don't like it when you say shit like that," Donna smiled.

"Too bad what you like. I know how to do my job. You want proof? You'll get proof. How I get it is none of your business."

"It is if you get it by illegal means," Donna said. "Don't get caught," she grinned.

Bank of America

1325 Main Street

Guilford, Connecticut

August, 2008

"Police," Harper said as she stood in front of the branch manager's lobby desk. "Stratford, and United States Attorney. I have a few questions for you."

"Let's talk," Jim Joseph said as he escorted Harper into his office. "What do you need?"

"I need you to explain why you ordered four hundred thousand dollars cash from the Federal Reserve in New York for a real estate transaction," Harper said.

"Oh, that," Jim said. "That was a routine transaction."

"There is no record of the transaction in the bank's computer," Harper said. "It has been erased."

"That has nothing to do with me," Jim said. "What's your point?"

"My point is that you have violated federal law. No paperwork was filed by you for this transaction. And don't give me that bullshit that they erased it, or I will erase you. I know what you did. Time to talk, Jimmy. They have backup records of cash shipments; I have those records. The money arrived here two years ago, and you signed for it. Talk to me, or you can spend the next twenty years in the joint."

"As I said, it was a standard transaction," Jim said, looking away. "Prove otherwise."

"And when I do?" Harper smiled. "You have a wife and three kids. Do you want them on welfare living in a homeless shelter after I have the government sell off all your assets? They'll love that. Come on, Jimmy. Fess up and I'll get you a good deal."

"You can't get me a good deal," Jim said. "This comes straight from the top. You either play ball or you die."

"There are worse things than death," Harper said. "Would you like to experience one of them?"

"You have no idea what you are up against here."

"Oh, but I do," Harper said. "And you know what the difference is between me and a little coward like you? I don't give a flying fuck for anything other than justice; not my life, not my job, not anything. Believe me when I tell you, if you don't cooperate, I will kill you deader than William Wallace. Talk to me."

"All right," Jim said. "But you have to help me."

"I will do what I can."

"Two words; Bartram Edwards. He set this up. It's his money, so it's his house no matter what the deed says. That girl he bangs signed a lot of shit at the closing, and I didn't get any copies."

"Write it," Harper said, throwing a pad on the desk. "Every detail. I'll be back in half an hour. Tanner Lee will keep you company."

Bank of America

1325 Main Street

Guilford, Connecticut

August, 2008

"Get your ass in there," Harper snarled, shoving Pereira into the office. The girl let out a string of curses in Portuguese, and spat at Harper.

"Uh oh; she's going to regret that move," Tanner Lee grinned.

Harper slapped the girl in the face hard enough to draw blood; she then kicked her in the groin and shoved her into a chair. "Now sit there and shut up, whore."

"Is that legal?" Jim Joseph said.

"It is if I say so," Harper said. "She tried to get away."

"Why is she here?" Joseph said.

"To corroborate your story," Harper said. "Ask her, kiddo," she said to Tanner Lee, who started questioning the girl in Portuguese. The girl nodded and looked away.

"Visto de turista," Harper said, holding out her hand. "Gimme." The girl handed over her Visa. "Expired over a year ago," Harper smiled. "It's just been revoked, and you with it." She called the local FBI office. "You're under arrest," she said. "Fucko el jail-o, or however you assholes say it. Tell her she has two choices; give us Edwards, or we'll give her to Edwards. After she testifies, it's hasta la vista baby. Back to Rio, and you can't get another Visa for ten years. Not that you'd want to, because you'd be dead before you could get out of the airport if you came back here." Tanner Lee repeated what Harper said.

"She understands."

"Excellent! Notarize her statement and get her out of here. Where's Clo-dog?"

"Cafeteria," Tanner Lee said.

"Oh. She could have invited us," Harper huffed. "And as for you, Jimmy, you're going into protective custody. Pack up."

"Now?" Joseph exclaimed.

"Yeah, now. Unless you want me to call Edwards' office and leave a message that you need a ride to the police station."

Office of the United States Attorney Donna J Melito

Eastern District of Connecticut at Bridgeport

Lafayette Boulevard, Bridgeport, CT

August, 2008

"This is better," Donna said as she spritzed herself with Chanel. "I can do this now. What's this?" she said, pointing at a red stain on the girl's affidavit.

"Tomato sauce," Harper grinned. "I can fix that. I'll have Tanner Lee retype that page. The Notary thingy is on the last page. We always do it that way in case …. you know, somebody spills something on the paper."

"You tune this babe up?" Donna said.

"She tried to escape," Harper said. "They all seem to do that. Give her a couple of weeks and she'll look good as new."

"Edwards is going to find out about this," Donna said. "He'll whack these three assholes."

"Not where I sent them," Harper said. "Remember Gary Busey's twin?"

"Oh, okay. He can't get to them there."

"Pereira will feel right at home; Friday is hooker night."

"There was a lot of good shit in those filing cabinets," Donna said. "Enough to get Edwards life."

"Death would be better, and more cost effective. You can have what's left of him after he gets out of Osborn," Harper said. "I think ten years in the worst African Nation cell block I can find should change his mind about a life of crime. I bet he looks nice in a wedding gown. Hey, did Tanner Lee find out where they stash all the dope?"

"Yeah; Mexico. We can reach out to their President, but you know how that goes."

"Yeah; no el find-o," Harper said. "World's biggest tag sale. That shit will be in the states within a week once they find out Edwards is out of the picture."

"Then we won't tell them," Donna said. "See if your friends can do anything about it. We know where the warehouse is; it's disguised as a sugar processing plant."

"Nose candy," Harper grinned. "I'll look into it. I have to go get a warrant from Brenda."

"What the hell is this?" Edwards said when Harper came in, flanked by three FBI Agents.

"You're under arrest is what it is," Harper said, holding up her badge. "Want a lawyer? Who cares; we aren't going to question you anyway. Stand up."

"Is this some kind of joke? Because if it is, you're all going to be sorry."

"You're the one who's going to be sorry," Harper smiled as she cuffed Edwards and searched him. She tossed a nine millimeter pistol to one of the Agents.

"That's a legal gun," Edwards snapped.

"Not in D.C. it isn't," the Agent said.

"Don't sweat the small stuff, Bart," Harper smiled. "We don't need the gun. We have enough without it. Move it. And no, you cannot make a phone call."

"State of Connecticut versus Bartram Edwards," the bailiff intoned. "Violation of State Banking Law, Money Laundering, Avoidance of the State Real Estate Tax Conveyance Statute, Conspiracy to Commit Tax Fraud, Bribery, two counts, Possession of a Controlled Substance with Intent to Distribute and or Sell, and Conspiracy to Harm a Minor. "

"Who represents the State?" Judge Allan Stevens said.

"District Attorney Brenda DiCenzo, Your Honor. Harper Cochran will second chair."

"And I see Rollins Canfield here," Stevens smiled. "You may as well just move in, Mr. Canfield. The state could use the rent money."

"I'm sure they could, Your Honor, but I have a home, thank you."

"How does the Defendant plead?"

"Not guilty. The defense requests reasonable bail. My client is a member of the U.S. House of Representatives."

"Like that's any reason to let him run loose," Brenda laughed. "The Defendant is facing a federal indictment, in which he's going to have to explain how he got over a billion dollars in drug money. You let this creep go, and all the witnesses will be in a dog food plant by sundown."

"Woof woof," Stevens grinned. "The Defendant is remanded without bail. Any pre-trial Motions?"

 "Move to dismiss all charges," Canfield said.

"You have lofty expectations," Stevens said. "Pick one."

"Let's start with Violation of State Banking Law; the People failed to state in the Complaint which law my client allegedly violated as required by the Practice Book."

"Brenda?" Stevens smiled.

"The People withdraw the charge," Brenda said.

"What else, Mr. Cannon?"

"Canfield, Your Honor. The money laundering charge is absurd. The Defendant merely transferred his own funds to a bank in Connecticut for a real estate transaction."

"Four hundred thousand dollars in cash ordered from the Federal Reserve," Brenda said. "The People maintain this money was the result of a criminal enterprise run out of the house the Defendant purchased. The cash was used by his girlfriend to purchase gold, silver, and platinum from local dealers. The metals were then shipped out of state and converted back into cashier's checks, which were deposited into a Bank of America account in Guilford, Connecticut. These funds were the source of the real estate transaction."

"It was still his own money," Canfield said. "You have no admissible evidence that he ever engaged in drug sales."

"A person is guilty of money laundering in the first degree when he exchanges or receives monetary instruments derived from felonious criminal conduct valued at more than $10,000 for other monetary instruments or equivalent property under CGS § 53a-276," Brenda said.

"That's money laundering in my book if Brenda can prove the drug charge," Stevens said. "Let the jury decide. Next."

"Conspiracy to Commit Tax Fraud and Avoidance of the State Real Estate Tax Conveyance Statute," Canfield said. "The Defendant was the purchaser, not the seller. Only the seller pays the conveyance charge."

"The seller fled the country," Brenda said.

"Smart man," Stevens said as the room laughed. "I should have done that the night before my wedding. I'm with Mr. Canfield on this one. Those two charges are dismissed. Any more?"

"The drug charges cannot attach to the Defendant. The drugs were found in a residence legally owned by Miss Pereira," Canfield said.

"A residence the Defendant paid for," Brenda said. "We got all the records from her running all over the state buying up precious metals for cash. She don't even have a job. She will testify as to where the drugs and money came from."

"The drug charges are in," Stevens said. "Have you discussed a plea agreement?"

"No," Canfield said. "The Defendant maintains his innocence."

"Okay; he can maintain it in Osborn Correctional. The Marshals will escort the Defendant. See the Clerk for a trial date. We are adjourned."

Stratford Police Department

900 Longbrook Ave.

Stratford, Connecticut

August, 2008

"Can you convict this clown?" Carole said, looking over the evidentiary report on Edwards.

"Yup," Harper said as she grabbed three pizza slices. "This is good pizza," she mumbled. "Vegetarian."

"I have to watch my weight," Carole said, looking up. "I have an image to uphold."

"So do the pigs at the Jimmy Dean sausage plant," Clodagh grinned. "And you know what happens to them. They wind up between some biscuits at the ShopMart."

"Shut up, Detective Potato," Carole snapped. "Or should I say patrolperson."

"You can say whatever the fuck you like," Clodagh said. "No Detective shield, no Clodagh. Don't forget, I know all about a life of crime, and I know where all this department's weaknesses are. I'm looking at the main one."

"Shit on you," Carole huffed. "Little Conan lookalike bastard. What do you use for hair conditioner?" Carole grinned. "Barbecue sauce?"

"At least I have hair," Clodagh said.

"I'm not bald!" Carole yelled.

"You aren't smart, either. You just read that file; did you see the evidence against this asshole?"

"I see it; but unlike you, I have experience. I've seen guys like this walk with more evidence than this against them. Bribery, intimidation, murder; one of them had a judge killed. He could get off."

"He could get off a tall building in the middle of the night in some hell hole city, too. He's not getting a walk, period," Clodagh nodded. "Not as long as I'm alive."

"That might be shorter than a quick stay at the Honeyspot," Carole said. "Everybody who works on this case has a target on their back. We are talking big time international drug dealing. Do you have any idea what these people will do to protect an operation like that?"

"Die," Harper smiled. "You of all people should know we will never let a piece of shit like Edwards get a pass, no matter who he bribes or tries to have killed. Even if he pulls it off, the day he walks out of that court house he will have crosshairs on his chest, and he will not walk away from that. Nobody does."

"I don't want a shooting war between my Detectives and some international drug gang," Carole said.

"Then go to work at Burger King," Harper said. "He goes, at any cost. My life, Clo-dog's life, your life. Period."

"Thanks," Carole said. "I didn't work forty two years here to get picked off in the parking lot by some dude named Mohammed."

"Then put in your papers," Clodagh said. "We don't need you."

Bridgeport Superior Court

Golden Hill St.

Bridgeport, Connecticut

August, 2008

"State of Connecticut versus Bartram Edwards," the bailiff intoned. "Money Laundering, Bribery, two counts, Possession of a Controlled Substance with Intent to Distribute and or Sell, and Conspiracy to Harm a Minor."

"Call your first witness, Brenda," Judge Stevens said.

"Call Maria Pereira," Brenda said. Maria took the stand and was sworn. "Permission to treat the witness as hostile," Brenda said.

"You haven't asked her anything yet," Stevens said. "Do you have a reason?"

"Miss Pereira is facing removal from the country for a Visa violation. The penalty is ten years before she can reapply. I want to make sure she is truthful."

"Okay, but don't go crazy," Stevens said. "Let's see what she has to say." The Court appointed translator spoke to Maria, who nodded.

"You speak English?" Brenda said.

"Yes."

"Who paid for the house you have been living in on the beach in Guilford?"

"This man," Maria said, pointing at Edwards.

"Let the record show the witness indicated the Defendant. What services did you perform for the DSefendant that resulted in this generosity?" Brenda said.

"Bangy bangy, and I sell narcotic for him."

"Bangy bangy?" Stevens laughed. "What's that?"

"Fucky sucky," Maria grinned. "He like to do a lot."

"Can't say that I blame him," Stevens sighed. "Continue."

"What kind of narcotic did you sell for the Defendant?" Brenda said.

"Cocaine and heroin. Also some LSD and Methamphetamine. This meth very strong, kill a lot of people."

"Objection," Canfield said. "There is no such evidence before the Court."

"Sustained. Just answer the questions, Miss Pereira. Don't embellish," Stevens said, looking away from Maria's legs.

"I no do this, I see people die use this product."

"The Defendant's product?" Brenda said.

"Yes. I give for man, he pay me twenty dollar. He do this," she said, indicating snorting. "He fall down two minutes later, policia come and look at him. I hide. Policia put coover over man like he dead."

"Coover?" Stevens said.

"Cloth, yellow, use for put over dead man. This man die fast."

"Request a continuance, Your Honor. This is new evidence the witness did not provide in her affidavit. The People may wish to amend their complaint based upon this evidence."

"Objection!" Canfield yelled. "This is ridiculous; the testimony of a law breaking kept woman should have no weight in this Court."

"My Detectives will investigate this alleged death," Brenda said. "If there ain't anything to it, the Defendant got nothing to worry about."

"Granted," Stevens said. "We will reconvene Monday next."

"Call Detective Jacqueline Jasper," Brenda said. Jackie was sworn and sat down. "Please tell the Court what your investigation uncovered."

"I interviewed Miss Pereira to get a good description of the decedent Raoul Perez. Her description matched the autopsy photos, and the Bridgeport Police verified that they were called to the scene at the time she indicated. The man was pronounced dead at the scene some ten minutes after the timeline Miss Pereira testified to."

"What was the cause of death?"

"Extreme toxicological reaction to methamphetamines," Jackie said.

"Tell the jury what that means in terms they can understand."

"Objection, Detective Jasper is not a toxicologist," Canfield said.

"She isn't testifying as one; she is merely interpreting the report," Brenda said.

"I'll allow it. No medical opinions, Detective."

"It means that whatever Miss Brazil over there sold him was not properly made. It contained too much of certain chemicals which stopped his heart. You need anything further, you get the Coroner to testify."

"What was the conclusion of your investigation, Detective?" Brenda said.

"I concluded that Maria Pereira sold a narcotic to Raoul Perez that caused his immediate death."

"I demand that Maria Perez be charged with the murder of Raoul Perez," Canfield said. "She admits to selling the narcotic that killed him; not the Defendant."

"The witness has been granted immunity in exchange for her testimony," Brenda said.

"Oh, sure; why not? Canfield laughed. "An alien who traded sexual favors for a nice house on the beach, and admits to selling a deadly narcotic that killed a man? Why shouldn't we believe such an upstanding person?"

"If the state granted immunity, it is beyond the power of this Court to undo it," Stevens said, "unless the defense can show evidence of corruption on the part of the District Attorney's Office or the police. Do you have such evidence, Mr. Canfield?"

"No, Your Honor, not at this time," Canfield said as Brenda glared at him. "But the Court should take notice of the fact that Miss Pereira's testimony was procured under circumstances that helped her avoid prosecution while implicating the Defendant with no evidence other than her word, which the prosecution paid dearly for."

"Duly noted," Stevens said. "Call your witness, Brenda."

"The people wish to continue examining Miss Pereira," Brenda said, smiling at Canfield. "I would remind Mr. Canfield that the people provided him with several new trial exhibits last Wednesday."

"I didn't see any new exhibits!" Canfield exclaimed.

"Not my problem," Brenda said. "Miss Pereira, what evidence do you have that confirms the Defendant provided drugs for you to sell?"

"Make movies," Maria said. "Show everything."

"Why did you make movies?"

"I afraid they blame me for this. I do for protect myself."

"What do the movies show?" Brenda said.

"Show man come to house, make delivery. Senhor Edwards pay him a lot of money. I see him do this."

"Objection," Canfield said. "This is all very entertaining, but it could have been Domino's for all she knows."

"Let's find out," Brenda said, holding up a remote as Edwards shook his head in dismay. She pointed the remote at a big screen TV and pushed the play button.

"No cartoons? I'm disappointed," Stevens sighed.

The video played for ten minutes; the quality was excellent. It showed Edwards taking delivery of two large cardboard cartons, and handing the other man a bundle of hundred dollar bills. He then put the boxes in a closet and locked it.

"Kind of says it all, doesn't it?" Brenda said. "Your witness."

"What was in those two boxes?" Canfield said.

"Narcotico," Maria said.

"I'm sorry, I must have missed the part where you opened the boxes and filmed the contents."

"No do this."

"Then no have proof," Canfield said. "All we have is your word. Why should we believe you?"

"I tell truth," Maria said.

"Sure, after you got a sweetheart deal from the prosecutor. Do you have any of the alleged narcotico left?"

"Yes. I no sell everything."

"People's 27," Brenda said. "Toxicology report on the contents of one of the boxes seized from Miss Pereira's home pursuant to a valid warrant. It isn't pizza, either."

"What is it?" Stevens said.

"Methamphetamine. It matches the drug found in the system of the man Miss Pereira sold to."

"Sounds like a good time for you to talk to Brenda, Mr. Canfield."

"Let's go, Sport," Brenda said, pointing at the conference room.

"You still can't connect those drugs to my client, try as you may," Canfield said. "I don't care what was in that box you tested. You cannot put it in my client's hands and you know it. You showed him taking delivery of two boxes; there is no way to prove that the box you tested was one of them. There is a big gap in your chain of custody of what you allege to be drugs."

"The only gap around here is between your ears, Canfield. If you think a jury is going to buy that line of crap you're selling, you're crazy."

"You lose this, your federal claim goes away too," Canfield said. "We will appeal if the jury makes the wrong decision."

"Appeals take a long time," Brenda said. "Meanwhile, Mr. Narcotico cools his heels in Osborn. That ain't the most pleasant place to vacation."

"We will demand protective custody if that happens, which I doubt it will. Face facts, Brenda; you can't make out a prima facie cases against my client."

"Then put him on the stand," Brenda shrugged.

"He doesn't have to testify," Canfield said.

"He doesn't have to go for a fitting for a push-up bra for the prison prom, either," Brenda said. "I'd like to hear what he has to say for himself; especially about where he got all that dough. He don't make that kind of money as a congressman."

"He saves his money," Canfield smirked. "Prove otherwise."

"I intend to," Brenda said. "I got more evidence to show the jury. You want to roll the dice? Be my guest. You got one offer, and one only; ten tears in state prison. Take it or leave it. You leave this conference room, the deal is off the table."

"No deal," Canfield said. "Go make your case. You already failed, but you won't accept that fact."

"Okay," Brenda shrugged. "Let's go. You too, asshole," she said to Edwards, who just smiled at her. "Let's see if you're still smiling when you got some convict's dick up your ass."

"I take it the negotiations failed?" Stevens said as court reconvened. Harper whispered something to Brenda.

"Correct," Brenda said. "The people are awaiting some evidence that will seal the deal on this dude. I didn't think we'd need it, but he ain't in the mood to cooperate. Request a continuance of one week."

"Objection," Canfield said. "It is obvious the people are stalling because they are not prepared. That is prejudicial to my client; he has to spend an extra week in prison because of the prosecution's incompetence."

"It's newly discovered evidence from Afghanistan," Brenda smirked, eyeing Edwards, who blanched visibly. "We got to deal with the State Department, which takes time."

"The continuance is granted, but this is the last one, Brenda. Get your ducks in a row."

"Quack quack," Brenda grinned at Canfield as she packed up. "You ain't gonna like what we got one bit. You're gonna wish you took that deal."

Stratford Police Department

900 Longbrook Ave.

Stratford, Connecticut

August, 2008

"Brenda wants you to go where?" Carole said.

"Afghanistan," Harper said as she grabbed a Cannoli. "That's where they make Afghans, right? Those are nice and warm. I'll bring a couple back with me for the house."

"You're insane; that's Taliban country. It's a war zone. What in the name of God does she want you to go over there for?"

"Escort a witness back here," Harper said. "The dude is facing execution for drug dealing if the Taliban catches him. They know who he is, and he wants out of the country."

"Execution for drug dealing?" Carole laughed. "In Afghanistan? Are you serious? That's like executing a Swede for making chocolate. The United States declared the poppy fields to be a no fly zone. That should tell you something."

"It does; Edwards and one of his pals in the government arranged for that. This guy we're bringing back is Edwards' supplier."

"You could get killed doing this," Carole said. "Those assholes play for keeps."

"I could get killed in Stratford," Harper said. "If I was worried about getting killed I'd be doing something else for a living. Besides, this should go nice and smooth."

"Us? Who else do you intend to take with you?"

"Carla, Tara, and me," Clodagh said as she commandeered a tin of Ziti and meatballs.

"No way," Carole said. "You aren't going over there."

"It's all set," Clodagh said. "Try to stop me."

"Your mother will choke me if anything goes wrong. Why are you doing this?"

"It's my job," Clodagh said. "Your job is to sit here and eat. End of discussion."

The Islamic Republic of Afghanistan

Taliban Headquarters

Kandahar

September, 2008

"You are Americans," Mohammed Omar said when Carla and Tara came in. "We are fighting you. Why are you here? I do not like Americans."

"This is a peaceful mission," Omar's second in command said. "You should listen to what they have to say."

"Americans are the cause of all the trouble here."

"We are here to extradite a man you would like to have killed, Mullah Omar," Tara said in Persian. "We need his testimony in court to convict an American congressman who imports opium into America. We would like to remove him to the United States peacefully."

"Who is this man you want?" Omar said.

"Sarwar Ghani," Tara said.

"Oh, him. There is a price on his head. What will happen to him after he testifies?" Omar said.

"Her," Tara said, pointing at Carla, who stared at Omar with a look that made him turn away.

"I see. Who are you?" he said to Carla.

"I am a police officer from a small town in America."

"You have death in your eyes," Omar nodded. "You will kill this man Ghani when you are finished with him?"

"Yes," Carla said. She took out her phone and showed Omar pictures of her stake burning victims. He nodded at her.

"This is an acceptable form of death for this man," he said. "What guarantees do I have that you women are telling the truth? Women are of no importance here."

"Allah has spoken to my heart," Tara said. "This man will die. You have my word."

Omar sat back for a long minute, then shook his head in dismay. "Girls," he sighed. "Who ever thought I would have to negotiate with girls. Take the man and go."

Office of the President of the United States

1600 Pennsylvania Avenue

Washington, DC

September, 2008

"How y'all doing?" G.W. grinned as Carla came in with Clodagh and Harper. Carla gave him a hug. "I remember you; you was here a few months ago. Y'all come here a lot. I like you gals. I am still the President, right?"

"Yes you are, G.W.," Carla said.

"Oh brother," Clodagh sighed. "How you doing, dude?" she smiled at G.W.

"That's me," G.W. beamed. "I got me a dude ranch in Texas. I am from Texas, right?"

"That's what they say," Carla smiled as they sat down.

"How's Barbara?" Harper grinned. "You fuck her lately?"

"She don't like that," G.W. said. "The flowers didn't work, neither. She hit me last time I tried."

"Try candy," Harper said. "Girls like candy."

"Will you stop?" Carla exclaimed. "Ev'ry time we come here, you tell the boy to do that. He cannot have sex with his mama."

"He can if he gets her the right present," Harper said. "I know; wait until she's asleep and stick it in her mouth."

"Stop!" Carla yelled. "Once more and I will beat your ass."

"You'll try," Harper said. "This time I'll be ready; not like the last time, you cheater."

"You gals want a soda?" G.W. said. "I got lots of soda."

"You ever have a lobotomy?" Clodagh said curiously.

"I don't think so," G.W. said.

"You don't think at all from the looks of things," Clodagh said.

"You two shut the hell up. Me and G.W. got business to corn-duct," Carla said. "I need me a favor."

"Executive Order?" G.W. said. "I like them. You write it up and I will sign it."

"I got it all writ up," Carla said, reaching into her bag. "We need a notary."

"Notary notary dock, Barbara sucked my ...." Harper sang.

"Shut up, damn it!" Carla yelled. "Don't pay her no mind," Carla said as she buzzed for G.W.'s secretary.

General Roland F. McHugh Jr., USMC

United States Central Command

MacDill Air Force Base

Tampa, Florida

September, 2008

"Is this real?" McHugh said. Carla looked down the front of her blouse.

"Oh, you mean the Order. It is," Carla said. "Y'all can call the White House and check it out."

"How does a small town police Detective get access to the President?"

"It's a long story," Carla said. "I got access to a lot of places. You ever meet General Cagney out west?"

"We aren't supposed to discuss him or his base," McHugh said. "You know him, too?" he laughed.

"Yup. Boy went to high school with my boss. 'Course there ain't nothin' worth a shit there," she grinned.

"I can imagine." McHugh called for a Major and handed him the Order. "Check this out, Cal," he said. "Would you ladies like something to drink?"

"Don't mind if I do," Carla said.

"What about me?" Clodagh said. "You got Irish whiskey, Sport?" she smiled at McHugh.

"Well, I'm not supposed to drink on duty," McHugh grinned. "And you look too young to drink."

"I'm forty," Clodagh said. "I look young for my age. Must be the Noxzema."

"You didn't get this from me," McHugh said as he took out a bottle of Jameson's.

"Carla's favorite expression," Clodagh grinned, poking her in the ribs. Ain't that right, cricket crotch?"

"Shut the hell up, you dirty mouthed redheaded midget," Carla snapped. "Don't pay her no mind," Carla grinned. "I am a cootie free gal. Y'all wanna see my squirrel?"

"Uh, no, that's all right."

The Major came back. "Checks out, Sir," he said. He winked at Carla and left.

"Boy likes me," she grinned. "I still got it."

"I thought the free clinic cleared that up for you," Clodagh said.

"Put a sock in it, you little bastard," Carla said.

"You two are funny," McHugh said. "This Order is not. It goes against stated foreign policy."

"G.W. makes foreign policy," Carla said. "Y'all enforce it. Policy just been changed," she said, pointing at the Order. "You got a problem with that?"

"G.W. can't tie his own shoes," McHugh said. "Who's behind this?"

"Me," Carla said.

"May I ask what this involves?"

"No, you may not. That is above your pay grade."

"I don't like ordering a mission like this without Congressional approval."

"The Corn-stitution says you do not need it, and you ain't gonna get it. G.W. is the Commander in Chief, and you ain't. He makes the rules, and y'all follow them. You want to keep this job, son? Mighty lonely shinin' Drill Instructors' boots on Parris Island."

McHugh downed his drink and poured another. Clodagh held out her glass. "Fill 'er up, Sport," she smiled.

"You could call me General," McHugh sighed as he poured.

"I could call you a lot of things," Clodagh smiled. "Like maybe Sergeant, after G.W. busts your ass. Or inmate, after you go to that nice prison in Kansas for disobeying a direct order from the President."

"I am from Kansas," Carla said as she slurped her drink. "You ain't gonna like it there."

"I didn't say I won't follow the Order; I said I don't like it."

"Who gives a shit what you like," Carla slurred as the whiskey hit her. She drained her glass and refilled it. "I risked my ass in Afghanistan while you sit on yours in a nice office. You will make them poppy fields disappear, or I will make you disappear. And I want film footage."

"Are you threatening me?" McHugh exclaimed.

"Nope. I am just stating a fact. Y'all wanna find out how much truth there is behind that fact? Or maybe I will just sic this miserable little bastard on you. I bet you'd enjoy that a whole lot."

"You got some nerve, coming in here and threatening a four star general."

"Like I said, it ain't a threat. You do your job and follow orders, and you will live to retire nice and peaceful like. Do it not, and …. well, shit happens." Carla stared at McHugh until he had to look away. "Good boy," Carla said as she put the bottle of whiskey in her bag and stood up.

"That's my whiskey," McHugh said.

"Not no more, it ain't," Carla said "Wanna try to take it away from me? Make ya famous," she grinned.

Stratford Police Department

900 Longbrook Ave.

Stratford, Connecticut

September, 2008

"Git in there, boy," Carla said as she shoved Sarwar Ghani into a holding cell. "Don't make no trouble, neither."

"You are girls," Ghani smirked. "I do not take orders from girls. I am a man."

"I'm a man, yes I am, and I can't help but love you so…" Harper sang. "Old people's music."

"What's this called?" Clodagh grinned as she hugged Carla.

"I give," Harper said.

"Holding the bag."

"You little …. Carla hissed. "I am gonna remember you done that. He's all yours," Carla said. "I got to finish up with the corn-struction dudes at the new po-lice station. I am gonna have a ce-ment statute of me made and put it out front," she grinned.

"They don't have that much concrete in the state," Harper muttered. "Bye." She went back to Ghani and sat down. "Let's go over your testimony," she smiled.

"I say what you want, then I go?"

"Yes," Harper smiled. "You go. I promise."

"Call Sarwar Ghani," Brenda said. "Attorney Cochran will conduct the examination." Ghani was sworn and sat down.

"Please tell the Court who you are and where you are from," Harper said.

"I am Sarwar Ghani. I am from Kabul, Afghanistan."

"What kind of work did you do in Afghanistan?"

"Opium processing and shipping," Ghani said.

"How much opium did you process in an average week?" Harper said.

"Thirty thousand kilos."

"Where did you ship it?"

"America."

"All of it?"

"Yes; all of it."

"Who paid you?"

"Him," Ghani said. "Edwards. Send money for me to Switzerland."

"What was the price he paid you?"

"Three thousand dollar American for one kilo."

"That's ninety million dollars a week, in case Canfield forgot his calculator," Harper said. "For how many years?"

"Five."

"That comes to 117 billion dollars street value according to the DEA," Harper said. "People's 37, affidavit of a DEA accounting official. Did you get to keep the ninety million per week?" Harper said.

"No. Have to pay government and tribal leaders. I get ten percent."

"Did Congressman Edwards ever tell you what he did with the Opium?"

"Process into heroin and sell to American addicts," Ghani shrugged. "You have big market here."

"And you are absolutely sure the Defendant is the person you dealt with."

"Yes, very sure. Have pictures when he come to Afghanistan."

"People's 38 through 52," Harper said as samples came up on the big screen TV. "Pictures of the Defendant posing with the witness. What is that behind you and the Defendant?" Harper said.

"One week opium production."

"Okay, let's discuss shipment. You were in charge of that, right?"

"Yes. I do shipping."

"Explain how shipment worked."

"Air Force put cargo ship on old runway at Bagram Air Base, north of Kabul. We send trucks and put product in airplane. Army provide guards. This big airplane; C130. Hold a lot. When full, it go. They put another airplane for us to fill."

"Did the Defendant ever say where the airplane landed?"

"Place call Mena Arkansas."

"And you personally saw the opium being loaded onto a United States Air Force cargo ship?"

"Yes. I help load."

"Did the Army guards know what was on the plane?"

"Yes. Sometimes we give them product."

"You realize that you contributed to the deaths of thousands of Americans, don't you?"

"No care for this," Ghani shrugged. "This no my problem. American want drug, we send."

"Nothing further."

Canfield stood up and looked at his notes.

"Are you under a death sentence in Afghanistan?"

"Yes. Taliban kill me if catch."

"Who arranged for you to come to the United States?"

"State Department. Tribal leader take me to talk to them."

"Why did you come here? To lie about the Defendant?"

"I come for get better life. No want to hide from Taliban all the time. I tell the truth."

"So let's be clear; are you going to be prosecuted here for drug crimes?"

"No. I do nothing illegal in United States. He do," Ghani said, nodding at Edwards.

"So you testify against a congressman with this fantastic tale, and you get to go free?"

"Yes."

"Why should we believe anything you say? It sounds like the government bought your testimony."

"No pay nothing. You think I lie? Explain pictures."

"Pictures can be faked," Canfield said.

"Objection," Brenda said. "He don't have any evidence these pictures are fake."

"Sustained. Watch the allegations unless you're prepared to prove them, Mr. Canfield," Stevens said.

"Why did you give opium to the Army guards?" Canfield said.

"Ask for this to smoke, to get high. No big deal," Ghani shrugged. "Have a lot. We give so they no talk."

"Did the Defendant ever personally touch the opium product when he was in Afghanistan?"

"No."

"Did he ever smoke it?"

"No."

"Did he ever personally hand you any money?"

"No. Do wire transfer."

"So, you get to keep all the opium money you made?"

"Yes."

"That's over 2 billion dollars. That's quite a payday for something you can't prove."

"Objection," Brenda sighed.

"Withdrawn," Canfield said. "Nothing further."

"Brenda?" Stevens smiled.

"Call Leonardo Bascutuccio."

"Easy for you to say," Stevens muttered. "We'll just call him Lenny."

Bascutuccio was sworn and sat down. "Mr. uh, Lenny, tell the jury what you do for a living."

"I am a financial analyst with the FBI. I also assist the CIA."

"Did you look into what Mr. Ghani just testified about?"

"Yes, I did."

"Please tell the Court what you found."

"Mr. Ghani provided me with the numbers for two Swiss bank accounts which contained some two billion dollars. Pursuant to our treaty with Switzerland where criminal activity is involved, the banks involved turned over all the records. I was able to trace the deposits back to the Defendant."

"Where did he transfer the money from?"

"Several accounts in the Cayman Islands."

"Are you sure the accounts were his?"

"Yes. No doubt whatsoever. The funds were transferred to the Caymans from a bank in Washington, D.C. and one in Guilford, Connecticut."

"What were the names on the accounts?"

"Edward Bartram on the D.C. account, and Maria Pereira on the Connecticut account."

"Are you sure it was Edward Bartram and not Bartram Edwards?"

"I'm sure," Lenny smirked. "Common mistake criminals always make. Also, he used his own social security number in Washington."

"What bank in Washington?" Brenda said.

"Bank of Georgetown. The manager's name is Bret Carlisle. It is a federally chartered savings bank."

"Not for long," Brenda grinned as she handed a paper to Harper, who got up and left. "Nothing further."

"No questions for the witness," Canfield sighed as Edwards fumed in his chair.

"The people rest," Brenda said.

"Any witnesses, Mr. Canfield?" Stevens smiled.

"Not at this time. Request a one week continuance to confer with my client."

"Denied," Stevens said.

"That isn't fair, Your Honor. The people got a week when they wanted it."

"Take it up on appeal," Stevens said. "If you have nothing further, I am sending the jury to deliberate."

"Brenda?" Canfield squeaked. "Is there still an offer on the table?"

"Nope. Told you I had the goods, but you wouldn't listen."

"Brenda called," Harper said as she looked at her new office. "Jury took five minutes; guilty on all counts. Sentencing is next month pending douche bag Canfield's appeal."

"Ain't gonna be no next month for that son of a bitch," Carla said. "I got plans for his ass. You got Ghandi or whatever the fuck his name is?"

"In the cruiser," Harper said. "Where do you want him?"

"Trunk of the Fairlane," Carla said.

"Amenia?"

"Yes," Carla said, looking out the window. "Why do they do it?" she whispered. "Stick that needle in their arm."

"Makes all the problems of the world go away," Harper shrugged.

"Never made my Ma's problems go away," Carla said, wiping an eye. "Just made 'em worse."

"I know, but you fixed all that. She's okay now."

"No she isn't," Carla said softly. "Can't bear to look at a man after what my Pa done to her. You call that okay? I wish that bastard was still alive so's I could kill him myself."

"Your mother has a good life now. She could have a man if she wanted one."

"She don't want one," Carla said. "She does not trust men."

"And you? Do you trust them?"

"Let's go," Carla said as she made for the door. "Put that bastard in the trunk. He got some serious sufferin' to do. I may not be able to kill my Pa, but I sure as hell can kill this no good cocksucker."

"Filthy disgusting skunk; I'm going to murder you," Harper said, a rag tied around her face. "I've had it with this. The next time you fart in the car, you will die the worst death you can imagine. Every time I go someplace with you, I have to put up with this."

"Y'all asked for it," Carla grinned. "You and Clo-dog, raggin' on my ass all the time, callin' me stupid."

"You *are* stupid," Harper snapped.

"Not as stupid as y'all," Carla said. "Usin' that rag you got tied around your ugly fuckin' face. I wiped my ass with that rag."

"Nooooooo!" Harper screeched. She started dry heaving and ran for the woods.

"She believes everything you tell her," Clodagh sighed as she took off her gas mask.

"That's what makes it so much fun," Carla said. She opened the trunk; Ghani stared at her in abject terror. His hands and feet were bound with duct tape.

"Where is this place you take me?" he squealed. "Other girl say I testify, then I go."

"Yeah," Carla grinned. "Although she didn't say where you were gonna go."

"Where ... where ... where ..." he stammered.

"Where, where, where, blah, blah, blah, fuck you," Carla said as she grabbed Ghani by the hair. "Out, motherfucker," she snarled as she dragged him out of the trunk and threw him on the ground.

"What you do to me?" Ghani cried.

"Kill you dead, you bastard," Carla nodded. "That's what you deserve. For the last five years, you made sure plane loads of that poison got delivered here to kill Americans. Almost 75,000 people here died from opiod overdoses in that five years, and you are responsible because you knew that shit was illegal poison. You ever shoot heroin or smoke that opium shit?"

"No," Ghani squeaked.

"Why not? It's good enough for Americans, but it ain't good enough for you?"

"He doesn't look too happy," Harper said as she came back.

"Fuck happy; he gonna be a lot less happy in about half an hour."

"Nooooooo!" Ghani screamed as Carla dragged him over to the cross on the ground.

"Untape his hands and hold 'em in place," Carla said with an evil smile as she held up her silver hammer and some railroad spikes. "We are gonna have us a barby-cue."

"That was awful," Clodagh said as Carla wended her way down Route 22 towards Brewster.

"Supposed to be," Carla said quietly. "God's punishment always exceeds the crime. Leastwise when I mete it out, it does."

"I never heard anybody scream like that before."

"You should hear Carla when she uses that battery powered dick in her desk," Harper snickered.

"I am gonna shove that dick up your chicken ass some day," Carla nodded. "Y'all love to disrespect me, don't you."

"It's a gift," Harper said. "You never answered the question I asked you before we left."

"What question?" Carla said as she watched the rear view mirror.

"Whether you trust men or not."

"I trust my friends and the men I work with. The rest ain't nobody's business."

"I bet you'd tell Christine if she asked you."

"We do not discuss men."

"You never give me the right answer," Harper sighed.

"That is because you never ask the right question. You keep pokin' your beak into my personal business over and over, expectin' a different result. You ain't gonna get one, so stop asking."

"You two sound like a Dr. Ruth show gone bad," Clodagh said. "Bunch of old biddies yapping at each other about who got laid the most last year."

"She did," Harper giggled. "At a damn good price, too."

"Better than gettin' fucked in the mouth by airline pilots for free," Carla said as she continued to watch the mirror.

"What are you looking for?" Harper said. "Your lost virginity?"

"Cops. They do not like me up here. Me and Vito broke just about every New York motor vehicle law there is. I do not want to get stopped smellin' of smoke."

"Then take a right onto 343 below Wassaic," Clodagh said. "There's a motel in Millbrook. We can all clean up."

"How in hell do you know what's in Millbrook?" Carla said.

"Unlike you, I prepare for trips like this. I scout out food joints, liquor stores, and motels. Oh, and bail bondsmen in case you get busted for the way you drive."

"I drive good," Carla said.

"Sure you do; just like Mario Andretti, and just as fast. You could star in one of those zombie apocalypse movies. It could be about a bunch of corpse eating assholes driving cross country in a '67 shit box Fairlane."

"You ain't as funny as you think you are," Carla said as she turned onto 343. Two miles later, she pulled into the parking lot of a western clothing store.

"Now what," Harper sighed. "Are you having a Kansas Hee-Haw flashback and need a new Stetson?"

"That ain't a bad idea," Carla grinned. "I think I will get me one of those, and some nice boots with spurs."

"Your mind is shot," Clodagh said.

"Less go," Carla said. "We ain't gonna clean up and then put the same stinky clothes back on."

They bought new clothes, checked into the motel in Millbrook, scrubbed themselves clean, dressed, and hit the road. Carla pulled into a pizza place and borrowed their dumpster. All the smoky clothes were in a big black Glad bag. She went inside, bought four large pizzas, and went back to the car.

"All right; food," Harper grinned. Carla held out her hand, palm up. Harper shook it. "Pleased to meet you, Dale," she giggled.

"Fuck you; pizza don't grown on trees. Cough it up."

"I don't have any money," Harper said. "I left it home."

"Y'all should have left your appetite home, too, you cheap bastard," Carla grumbled.

They were approaching Wingdale when a town cruiser pulled out of a strip mall and hit the light bar. Carla pulled over and waited. A big cop walked up to her window and looked inside.

"I know who you are," he grinned.

"Is that so?" Carla said. "I do not know you. What do you want?"

"This car is on our hot list. That means you have a reputation for speeding, among other things."

"Was I speeding just now?" Carla said.

"No."

"Then fuck off, Gomer. I outrank your ass somethin' awful," she said, holding up her state and federal badges.

"Motor vehicle stuff isn't a federal beef, and this ain't Connecticut," the cop said.

"No shit, Sherlock," Carla said. "You can fuck off anyway. We got places to go and things to do. Hold me up for no good reason, and I will have you indicted by the feds for obstruction. Don't think I can't do it, either."

"She can," Harper grinned. "You should let her go; she's clinically insane. She has cooties, too."

"License and registration," the cop said.

Carla quickly held out her paperwork, then stuffed it into the glove box. "I am leaving, since you got no probable cause for your little traffic stop. Bye." She put the Fairlane in gear and roared away. The cop ran to his cruiser and pursued her, but she was so far ahead of him he gave up after half a mile.

"They'll be waiting for you on I-84 at the state line," Clodagh said.

"Good. I ain't using I-84."

She headed south, and got onto I-684. She got off in Katonah, and took Rte 35 into Ridgefield. She continued on until she came to Rte. 7, and headed south. In Norwalk, she jumped on I-95 and headed north to Stratford.

"How's that," she grinned as they pulled into the P.D. parking lot. "Didn't even speed."

"He got your plate number, dipshit," Clodagh said.

"Oh, that," Carla said as she took out a screwdriver. "That be a stolen plate, and I had my thumb over the real plate number when I showed him the reggie."

"You really expect to get away with this?" Clodagh said.

"Get away with what? Boy said I done nothing wrong, and I got witnesses. That would be you."

"It would be me if I got taken out to dinner," Harper grinned.

"How about if you just get taken out?" Carla said, pointing at her Colt.

"You'd shoot me over a traffic bust?" Harper exclaimed.

"I'd shoot you just for the fun of it," Carla grinned. "Where you want it? Leg, arm, or ass?"

"You'll have to kill me so I can't talk," Harper said. "Dinner beats a murder rap."

"Damn, you are a connivin' little bastard. Let me change my plate and hide this car, check in with Methuselah, and we will go eat."

Ten minutes later, they looked into Carole's office. She was asleep at her desk, a string of drool hanging from her chin.

"I ain't goin' near that," Carla said, backing up. "Less go eat. Fuck checkin' in."

"Why do old people drool when they sleep?" Harper said as they left.

"Ain't got nothin' else to do," Carla shrugged. "Cept wait for the Grim Reaper."

"She isn't that old," Clodagh said. "Is she?"

"She's sixty," Carla said.

"What's the life expectancy in Connecticut?" Clodagh said.

"Fifty nine," Harper giggled.

"Carla is 145," Clodagh smiled. "If you believe her horse shit reincarnation stories."

"Fuck you," Carla said. "I will kill your ass and myself, we will be reincarcerated, and I will find you and kill your ass again."

"Get out," a Marshal said to Edwards as he opened the rear door of the SUV.

"We're only halfway to the entrance," Edwards said.

"What, you in a hurry?" the Marshal smiled. "I gotta take a piss. Stand by the front of the car so I can see you." He walked over to the trees alongside the road and unzipped.

"Don't they have bathrooms for you guys in this dump?" Edwards called out.

"Yeah, but they ain't that clean."

While he urinated, the Marshal was contemplating the twenty thousand dollars he had found in a paper bag on the front seat of his personal vehicle that morning with a little map drawn in crayon. "Park and piss hear take your time put him outside the car" was scrawled across the bottom. He had laughed at the childish scrawl and misspelled word, but the cash took his mind off the note. All used hundreds, non consecutive serial numbers.

"You done yet?" Edwards called out. "It's starting to ....." The word "rain" never escaped his lips. He was struck in the face by a fifty caliber explosive round, which effectively removed his entire head. The corpse jerked and staggered around, spurting blood, then fell over. The Marshal got on the radio and called it in.

Nine hundred yards away, Flannery and Debbie waited on the roof of an abandoned building and radioed CIA Ricky, who picked them up a few minutes later with his MH-6 Little Bird "Killer Egg" helicopter.

"Good shot for an amateur," Debbie giggled as she poked Flannery in the ribs.

"Stop poking me, or I'll throw you out of this piece of junk," Flannery said.

"You'll try," Debbie said. "You can't beat me in a fight."

"Who said anything about a fight?" Flannery grinned. "I'll shoot you in that cinder block you call a head, then I'll throw you out."

"Hey," Ricky said. "No shooting in my helo. You might hit something vital."

"Shoot him in the nuts," Debbie giggled. "I can fly a helicopter."

"He said something vital," Flannery said. "That lets out his nuts, and his head."

"You two are a riot," Ricky said. "You got my money?"

"Yeah, and I'm keeping it," Flannery grinned. "Debbie and I are going shopping for trashy lingerie."

"Oh; you get a new mule or something?" Ricky laughed. "Put a negligee on it. Probably look better on the mule than it would on you."

"Just fly the ship, dickless wonder," Flannery said. "The check is in the mail."

The Islamic Republic of Afghanistan

Badakhshan Province

October, 2008

"CASINO 53 to Central Command," B-52 pilot Major Jim Roland said into the mike. "Approaching target. Confirm mission."

"Confirmed," Central Command said. "Execute."

"Roger," Roland said. "Get ready, Pete," Roland said into his headset.

"Roger," Captain Pete Mansfield, the Electronic Warfare Officer said. "Say when."

"Target approaching in five seconds," the Co-pilot said. "In four, in three, in two, in one, target acquired.

"When," Roland said into the headset.

Pete released the payload of seventy Mark 79 one thousand pound incendiary bombs.

"Where the hell did they find these antiques, Major?" Pete laughed.

"It is not for us to question the origin of our ordinance," the Major said. "We just deliver it. That aside, there is a certain Colonel at Barksdale who has been around since the Revolutionary War. It is said he can find just about anything."

"I'm glad that stuff is out of the ship," Pete sighed. "Shit looked pretty unstable."

Roland banked away at 40,000 feet and headed for Bagram to refuel. Beneath him, he saw a series of brilliant flashes as the poppy fields where Edwards' opium supply had come from were vaporized in a huge cloud of flames.

"There are supposed to be Army dudes guarding those fields, you know," the Co-pilot said.

"Hey," Roland shrugged. "You lay down with pigs, you get up smelling like Madonna, or some shit like that. Fuck 'em. You want to guard the government's opium, you take your chances."

"Yeah," the Co-pilot sighed. "I got a cousin who overdosed on that shit. That's why I put in for this mission."

"This is a secret mission," Roland said. "By order of G.W. himself. Don't talk in your sleep."

"Roger that, Captain. I don't even remember getting up this morning."

Stratford Police Department

900 Longbrook Ave.

Stratford, Connecticut

October, 2008

"What did you assholes do now?" Carole said the next morning. "Some townie from Wingdale, New York called. Seems you ran on him."

"I did not run on nobody," Carla said. "Boy stopped me; said I was on some list for bein' a law violatin', speed crazed son of a bitch. I asked him if I had been speeding before he stopped me, and he said no, so I left."

"He didn't give you permission to leave," Carole said.

"I didn't ask for any; didn't need it. Boy said I were innocent as charged, so I booked. Fuck him if he don't like it. I got better things to do than jaw jack with some Barney Fife lookin' creep like him."

"You love to do this, don't you," Carole sighed. "Make trouble for the department."

"I take full advantage of my rights. If that boy don't like what I done, he can come down here and settle this the old fashioned way."

"Just what we need; the murder of a cop on police property."

"Nobody is gonna get killed. Less the boy gets out of corn-trol," Carla grinned. "Send him an invite, and we will see what he got in his panties other than shit stains."

"Look who's talking," Clodagh muttered. "Miss Brown Streaks herself."

"I will do no such thing," Carole said. "Ignore this; just stay out of wing nut, or whatever it's called. Where is that, anyway?"

"Route 22 in Jew York," Carla said. "You old hippies used to go up there all the time when they had Dover Drag Strip open."

"Oh, okay. I know where that is. What were you doing up there?"

"Driving home," Carla said.

"From where?" Carole said, leaning back in her chair.

"Wherever I was before I was in Wingdale."

"And where would that be?" Carole said.

"It wouldn't be," Carla said. "Unless it was, which it ain't."

"Here we go," Clodagh said. "The Abbott and Costello routine. I'm out of here; I need breakfast."

"Me too," Harper chirped.

"Me three," Carla said. "Let the coffin dodger get her own damn breakfast."

Kirisawa's Japanese-American Diner

Stratford Avenue

Stratford, Connecticut

October, 2008

"I don't know about comin' here," Carla said. "Last time we was here I shot me a damn nigger cop."

"You what?" Clodagh exclaimed. "You shot a cop?"

"Do I stutter? Boy drew on me. Wasn't a real cop, just one of them half assed Australian cops. Besides; they got plenty of niggers in Norwalk, where he was from. One less won't make no difference."

"Australian?" Harper giggled. "You mean auxiliary."

"Whatever. That were last March, and I ain't heard a word about it from nobody. Fucker cost me three grand to get rid of the body, too. Damn Jap dump be bad luck. Maybe I will shoot that bastard cook Haruto next."

"How the hell did you get away with killing a cop?" Clodagh exclaimed.

"Easy. Nobody in here would say nothin'; besides, it were self de-fense. Boy drew first and did not identify himself as a po-lice officer. Prob'ly too fuckin' stupid to remember he be a cop instead of bein' chased by one. Harper seen it go down. She is my witness; and Flannery, too."

"I may develop a conscience and testify against you," Harper grinned. "Unless you pay for breakfast, that is. There is no statute of limitations on murder."

"I didn't murder nobody," Carla snapped. "And I already got me a statue on order for the new station," she grinned. "Ain't no limitation on how big it can be, neither. And murder don't apply to niggers, only humans."

"Is there any way we can get rid of her?" Clodagh whispered to Harper. "I'll pay Jimmy the Drunk's fee."

"I have commitment papers at the station," Harper said. "We can have her slobbering and drooling on herself in some nut house by sundown. Then again, we'd have to pay for our own food if we did that."

"Forget it then," Clodagh said. "Wait until she runs out of money. I still don't believe you shot a cop, Carla," Clodagh sighed. "And the nigger remarks are out of line. We are supposed to be neutral and unbiased. Is there any group of people you like?"

"Swedes and Germans," Carla grinned. "They got big ….."

"Enough," Harper said, "Miss bigot. A lot of Germans are Jews. We all know you don't like them, either."

"I got nothin' agin them cheap bastards," Carla huffed. "That gal Ruth at the Jew Pastry Shop on Paradise Green ain't a bad sort, although I think she got one of them trick cash registers that adds twenty percent. We got to check that out. And real Germans are from Austria; not Is… Is …."

"It is what it is," Harper keened.

"Yeah, that's it. That shitty little country next to all the A-rabs. Why we got to give them bastards billions of dollars? Too fuckin' cheap to defend theyselves. And do not tell me they are poor."

"You should work for the United Nations," Clodagh said. "Either that or be executed in public. Let's take a vote."

Waitress Betty Lou came over. "Want food?" she said.

"No; we came here to admire the decor," Harper said. "Like the picture of the Arizona in flames behind the counter. Of course we want food."

"Haruto no like Carla," Betty Lou said. "Him say she order crazy shit nobody can cook, and she say she shoot him."

"Fuck him," Carla said. "If that old bastard shows me his wrinkly old hind end again, you will be lookin' for a new cook."

"Moon over Mitaka," Betty Lou giggled.

"Who?" Carla said.

"Mitaka. This Japanese city."

"Thought we bombed all them cities," Carla said. "You mean you got one left?"

"Have a lot. Order food, cheap prostitute."

"Fuck you, Tokyo Rose. I am an expensive prostitute."

"Spell it," Harper grinned.

"H-O-R-E," Carla grinned. "I kin spell, and I kin cipher, too."

"What's 200 with twenty percent off," Clodagh said.

"Discount blowjob," Carla said as she watched the parking lot in front. "Here we go," she sighed as two men got out of an old Chevy. "Two dudes with guns. Looks like a stickup."

"The guy with the shaved head and the spider tattooed on his skull is cute," Harper said as she took out her Python.

 "How do you know they have guns, Columbo?" Clodagh said.

"Because it is my job to know," Carla said as she took out a .45.

"I thought you only used that old six shooter," Clodagh said.

"The automatic version gives me a little variety," Carla said as she slipped the big Colt under her napkin. "You packing?"

"Nope. Can I fuck with them? Pretty please?"

"After I disarm their asses," Carla said as the men came in and sat down. They looked around disinterestedly and paid no attention to the girls. Carla got up and headed for the door. "Be right back." She went to the trunk of the Fairlane then came back inside, her hands behind her back. "Hey boys," she called out. They turned around. "Ever see one of these?" she grinned, taking the B.A.R. out from behind her back.

"Jesus!" one man yelled. "What the hell is that?"

"Model 1918 Browning Automatic Rifle. Fires a 30.06 cartridge, twenty rounds. Wanna see what ten of 'em in your ass feels like, fuck face?"

"Watch your mouth, bitch," the man scowled. "You ain't got the balls to fire that gun."

"Wrong thing to say to her," Harper whispered.

"Take that gun out of your waistband real slow," Carla grinned. "Now." The man reached for the gun; Carla stitched him from his crotch to his throat with the B.A.R. He slumped to the floor in a pool of blood. The other man made a quick draw move; it was his last. Carla gave him the rest of the magazine in the chest.

"You make big mess!" Betty Lou yelled. "Every time copper come here, kill somebody!"

"Boys was gonna rob your dumb ass," Carla said. "You rather we had just up and left you here?"

"Asshole," Betty Lou grumbled. "Who clean up all this blood?"

"Not me," Carla said as she changed magazines. "I do the shootin', you do the cleanin'. Them's the rules." She went back to the table. "And I expect breakfast, too. No little thing like this should stop y'all from servin' folks. Call it in, pipsqueak," she grinned at Clodagh.

"What a fucking trigger happy moron," Clodagh laughed as she called the station.

"Boys drew on me," Carla said. "Y'all seen it with your own two beady little eyes."

"The gun is still in his waistband."

"Oh; I kin fix that." Carla went over to the man, removed the gun from his pants, and dropped it next to him. She went back to the table and sat down. "That'll teach his ass to fill his hand agin the best there is."

"Welcome to Stratford," Harper chirped. "Land of the stupid and home of the riddled with bullets."

"I am gonna have us a new slogan on them cruisers I ordered," Carla said. "Fuck that protect and serve bullshit. Ours is gonna say shoot first, ask questions later. Clo-dogh, go see if them boys got any money. Ammunition ain't cheap."

The Orion Motorcar Company

Lordship Boulevard

Stratford, Connecticut

October, 2008

"Thank you for seeing me," Governor Dan O'Herlihy said.

"You're welcome," Christine said. "I don't remember you; how did you become Governor?"

"That really isn't important, is it?" O'Herlihy smiled. "Just mundane politics. One man resigns, another man takes his place."

"In other words, you were not elected to your current position, correct?" Christine said.

"Well, technically I don't have to be. Does it bother you that I'm the Governor?"

"No, but the week isn't over yet. What do you want?"

"I wanted to give you a heads up," O'Herlihy said. "I'm letting several of the biggest businesspeople in the state know what to expect from Hartford."

"Gee, how nice of you," Christine smirked. "Let me guess …. you're cutting the corporate tax rate."

"Good one," O'Herlihy laughed. "Actually we're leaving it the same. We are, however, submitting legislation to create a new financial oversight board to monitor profits in businesses of …. your type, and adjust them accordingly."

"My type?" Chistine said. "Do you mean automotive businesses?"

"No; I mean … successful businesses. Our constituents feel that you make too much money."

"The opinion of your constituents, who would be looters, means nothing in this office. What I make is none of their concern."

"They feel otherwise."

"Their feelings count as much here as do their opinions."

"The new office won't concern itself with politics or feelings."

"I imagine not; just profits, and how much money they can confiscate," Christine smirked. "This is the sort of thing the old Soviet Union used to do. Glad to see the concept is still alive and well in the Democrat Party."

"Republicans in the Legislature will support this effort too."

"All four of them?" Christine laughed. "I bet they will, as long as they get their cut. What's in it for me, other than being stuck with the check?"

"You shouldn't think of it that way," O'Herlihy said.

"And you shouldn't think of it at all. In plain simple terms that even you can understand, I refuse to pay."

"Refuse what? The bill isn't even written yet. You don't know what it will say."

"Oh, I know what it will say," Christine nodded. "I've seen other bills you grifters passed. This one will not fare any better. My check book is not a tool you may use to cure your spending deficits."

"You should consider your social obligation," O'Herlihy said as he pulled at his collar.

"Hot in here, isn't it," Christine grinned. "I'd consider my social obligation if I knew what it was, other than to produce a superior product at a competitive price. Perhaps you can enlighten me."

"I wasn't expecting this level of resistance," O'Herlihy said.

"I know," Christine said. "Fun, isn't it? Especially since there isn't a damn thing you can do about it. I've been through this before, you know, and here I sit."

"You sit here because we let you," O'Herlihy said. "Don't make the mistake of thinking otherwise."

"I sit here because I paid for this plant, and it is mine to do with as I see fit. That does not include being raided by a bunch of corrupt politicians."

"Are you insinuating that I am corrupt?" O'Herlihy said.

"What you are speaks so loudly that I have no need of hearing what you say. Hear this, Mr. O'Herlihy, and hear it well; you will never get one nickel more from me than I currently pay. I will relocate, dynamite this plant, and give the land to a Church where it will be beyond your grasp before I will accede to your corrupt demands and extortion."

"This is a nice plant," O'Herlihy said, looking around. "It would be a shame to lose it."

"I have enough money to build ten plants like this," Christine said. "And that money is in a place where you'll never get your grubby paws on it. If you don't think I'll do it, go ask the former Governor of New York; you know, the one who killed himself when we moved to Georgia and deprived him of half his revenue."

"But Miss Connor; you don't understand why we are doing this. That's your problem."

"No, it is your problem that I *do* understand why you are doing this. And I am here to tell you it will fail."

"There are ways to bring businesspeople into line," O'Herlihy said. "You may not like them, either."

"Neither will you when you see the results of your efforts," Christine said. "You are going up against something you do not and cannot ever understand."

"What I understand is that you worship money like it was a God."

"You understand nothing," Christine said. "To you, money is something to be confiscated and used to fund your failed Utopian social projects. You justify the seizure of other people's money by convincing yourself that it is for the public good; minus your cut, that is. We who earned it have a different view. Money is the result of success; it is a free country's reward to us for what we produce. You, on the other hand, produce nothing but misery and despair. When you finally figure that out, it will be too late for you."

"Why?"

"Because you have no clue as to who or what you are taking on. We who are the titans of business, as you call us, exist for one purpose; ourselves."

"How noble of you."

"It is, but I would never expect a dullard like you to understand why. Free men work for their own benefit; the reason is immaterial. You would have them work for the benefit of strangers who hug their mattresses all day, depending on receiving someone else's money through your extortionate laws in exchange for their vote. When we refuse to pay up, you don't know what to do."

"I can have your face plastered all over every network by the end of the week," O'Herlihy smirked. "You'll be the new Queen of Mean."

"I couldn't care less; I only care about my customers. The bums who watch your liberal TV networks couldn't afford a bicycle, much less one of my cars."

"Snooty millionaires buy your cars; is that all you care about?"

"The Orion is priced a notch below the mid range cars of the Big Three; hardly millionaire territory. The snooty millionaires buy my father's cars," she smirked. "I bet you'd like to have one, but you can't afford it unless you steal more money and take more bribes."

"All right, we can argue about cars all day, but in the end you'll pay your fair share of that new program, and you'll be glad to do so."

"You aren't listening; no more money, not now, not ever. If you don't like it, do something about it. I know I will."

"Tell me what you'll do," O'Herlihy smirked. "I'd like to know."

"No. Find out the hard way, you cheap hack. Now get the hell out of my office, and don't ever come back."

"I'm going to remember this conversation," O'Herlihy said as he stood to go. "And you will be the focus of my attention for the next several months."

"And you will be mine," Christine said. "Let's see who comes out on top."

After the Governor had left, Christine called Carole. "I need Tanner Lee to do some research for me. How much shall I pay you?"

"Is this a police matter?" Carole said.

"Not yet, but it might be. It involves another shake down by the Governor of Connecticut. It will get nasty and people will get hurt, I promise you."

"Oh, so now you need us?" Carole smirked.

"I said I'm willing to pay."

"She makes sixty thousand a year. Divide accordingly. Make the check payable to the Town of Stratford." The line went dead in Christine's hand.

"Miserable, fat pizza gobbling slug," Christine muttered as she slammed down the phone.

The Orion Motorcar Company

Lordship Boulevard

Stratford, Connecticut

October, 2008

"What do you need?" Tanner Lee smiled. "I have limited time for this."

"Thank you for coming. I need to know what the state of Connecticut purchases that is automotive related, and who they purchase it from."

"That's all on the state web site," Tanner Lee said. "It is required disclosure under state law."

"It is gone," Christine said. "I looked yesterday. It says there is some sort of internet problem, check back later."

"Oh, that one," Tanner Lee said. "They always do that when they want to hide something. What is this about?" Christine related the details of her visit with the Governor. "Oh, him," Tanner Lee said with a wave of her hand. "A complete failure who has good political connections to other failures. He has never held a job in the private sector, and he has been the subject of several corruption investigations, all of which were dismissed by his own party. He is a despicable, disgusting, revolting excuse for a human, which is a rather high bar to accomplish considering how low humans can go."

"You don't like your own kind very much, do you," Christine said.

"No, I do not. Can you blame me?"

"No, I cannot. That is why you are here."

"What do you want to do to Mr. O'Herlihy?" Tanner Lee said.

"Ruin him," Christine said as she looked out her office window. "Irrevocably and permanently. And not through violence, either This man deserves to be extinguished by that which he hates most; honest commerce by honest, free men trading their wares in the free market. I want to bring the full force of the free market against him."

"It isn't as free as you think it is," Tanner Lee said.

"Then we will make it so," Christine snapped. "It used to be; it can be so again. The interference of rat moochers and horrid little men like O'Herlihy cannot stop the collective minds of free men. We refuse to be ruled."

"Better have some bulletproof underwear, lady," Tanner Lee nodded. "These are tough people. Sometimes violence is all they understand."

"I will not resort to violence to achieve business success," Christine said. "All my life, I have lived by one code; I am better at what I do than anyone else, and I will succeed because of my own efforts. I will not succeed by committing murder; that's what they do."

"Okay," Tanner Lee sighed. "I've been a cop for a while, and I see how people operate. I don't approve of it, because I was raised in a better place than this. The problem I have is that I have seen how humans operate, and I don't like or understand it. However, I am somewhat bound by the law I swore to uphold. In the human world, violence works. It is quick and effective."

"No violence. I have staked my life on my ideas, and if they are wrong it is my burden to accept the consequences. They are not wrong; you will see that if you do what I want."

"Okay," Tanner Lee said. "The battle is yours. I will get you the information you require. What is it you really want?"

"I want to be known as the woman who took down the government of the State of Connecticut."

"You have lofty goals," Tanner Lee said.

"I've always had them," Christine said. "And I have never abandoned them. That's why I am where I am."

"Okay," Tanner Lee sighed. "Let's do it. If this blows up in your face, I can get you a position making cars in the Pleiadian Star System."

"I bet I can make better cars than they have now," Christine grinned.

"You really need to talk to a shrink," Tanner Lee sighed. "Do you have a computer I can use?"

"Take the office next to my secretary's; it has three."

"This is going to get very nasty for you," Tanner Lee said. "These people will stop at nothing. Maybe you should wait and see just how much this new tax will cost you."

"You cannot feed the beast; you must slay it," Christine said.

"You're only one person," Tanner Lee said.

"Sometimes that's all it takes," Christine smiled. "Besides; Carla will help me, as I have helped her."

"You helped Carla? How?"

"I cannot discuss that, but I assure you she will stand with me. We have similar beliefs."

"You're some kind of atheist according to Carole; Carla makes the Pope look like an agnostic."

"I didn't say what beliefs we have in common," Christine said. "They do not involve religion."

"Okay," Tanner Lee shrugged. "Give me a couple of days." She turned and went to her new office.

The Orion Motorcar Company

Lordship Boulevard

Stratford, Connecticut

October, 2008

"I have a preliminary list of vendors," Tanner Lee said. She tossed the printout onto Christine's desk. "Oh, by the way; your printer needs ink cartridges."

"In the storage closet in the corner of the office," Christine said as she looked at the printout. "This is good; I can do a lot of damage with this."

"You can do damage with a list of vendors?"

"Of course," Christine smiled. "Watch me. And if I can't, there is a man out there who can."

"Who?" Tanner Lee said.

"I don't know; nobody really knows who he is, but he is out there. He seems to appear when you need him."

"Sounds like Superman," Tanner Lee smiled.

"Some have said that about him. Myself, I have never used his services. I don't even know how to contact him or who he is. Most say you don't have to; he will find you. Okay, let's see; the state currently purchases all its cars from eight Ford dealerships around the state; let's put a stop to that."

"How?" Tanner Lee said.

"Why, I'll buy them all and convert them to Orion dealerships," Christine smiled. "I'll make them an offer they can't refuse."

"They'll just get new dealers," Tanner Lee said.

"I'll fix it so they can't. I am in the car business, you know. I can do anything I want."

One hour later, Christine hung up her phone and went into Tanner Lee's office. "Done," she said. "I just spent eighty million dollars, and we have 8 new Orion dealerships. I should recoup my investment in less than two years."

"What about them finding new Ford dealerships?" Tanner Lee said.

"They won't be able to," Christine grinned. "The district manager for the state used to work for me on the Monarch assembly line. It seems the state's credit has been downgraded by a man who also worked for Monarch, and they are a bad risk. There will be no further sales. The state has a five year contract with Ford; it requires good credit. They have defaulted on that agreement, and will have to pay off Ford to the tune of twenty million dollars for cars they cannot buy. Let's see how they like that."

"You're a real bitch," Tanner Lee laughed.

"You haven't seen anything yet," Christine smiled. "I'm just getting started. I built something of great value by using the power of my mind. Let's see how the moochers like it when I turn that power against them."

Office of the Governor

State Capitol

Hartford, Connecticut

October, 2008

"What do you mean we can't buy any cars?" O'Herlihy roared.

"Our credit has been cut off," the Comptroller, Mary Hawley, smirked. "We are deadbeats."

"We need eighty new cruisers for the State Police!" O'Herlihy exclaimed. "You have to fix this. Contact those dealerships at once."

"They have been sold," the Comptroller said.

"Which ones?"

"All eight of them."

"To whom?"

"Orion Motorcars. They are changing the signs as we speak."

"That no good ….. you call Roberts, the Ford district manager. You fix this."

"I did call him; who do you think told me our credit is no good?"

"We are a sovereign state; the richest one in the country. How dare some creep tell me our credit is no good! Hello? Are you there?" The line had gone dead in the Governor's hand. "I will have that fucking whore killed," O'Herlihy hissed. "She can't get away with this." He got back on the phone and buzzed his secretary. "Get me the district manager for Chevrolet," he snapped.

"Oh, hello, Governor," former Monarch employee Rand Elliott smiled as he put the call on speaker phone. "What can I do for you?"

"I would like to order eighty new cruisers for the State Police. I need them right away."

"Oh, that's unfortunate," Rand said as he pumped his fist up and down in his lap to the glee of his sales staff. "I'm afraid I can't help you."

"What do you mean you can't help me?" O'Herlihy squeaked. "I need those cruisers!"

"Well, first of all, your state's credit has been downgraded to a status skunks in my back yard exceed. Also, we have a non-compete agreement with Ford and Chrysler where government is concerned. You still have a contract with Ford, the terms of which you have not satisfied. I cannot sell you anything until you settle up with them; it's twenty million or so as I recall."

"You rotten no good son of a bitch," O'Herlihy hissed. "You wait until you see what happens to you." The line went dead.

"I think you should be the one who worries about that," Elliott sighed as he hung up. "You bit off more than you can chew this time."

"What the hell is going on!" O'Herlihy yelled to his secretary. "This is an outrage! Call the President! I'll show these bastards what real power is about. And get Toyota on the line. Those Jap bastards would do business with the devil."

World Headquarters, USA, Toyota Motor Corporation

President of USA Operations, Akihiro Takanami

Philadelphia, Pennsylvania

October, 2008

"Oh, hello, Governor," Akihiro said. "What can I do for you?"

"I need eighty police cars," O'Herlihy said. "And I need them this month."

"We do not build police cars," Akihiro said. "So sorry."

"You ….. you can do this. I have the blueprints."

"We cannot," Akihiro said. "This involves changes to our assembly line, perhaps a new plant. There is no demand for Toyota police cars."

"How much would a new plant cost?" O'Herlihy said. "I'll pay."

"Three hundred million dollars," Akihiro said. "You have cash? We will produce your cars in two years."

"Two years? Why so long?"

"Take long time to build factory. We no do this without long time contract. You want to order three hundred million dollars' worth of police cars?"

"I can't do that," O'Herlihy said. "Nobody can do that."

"Then good-bye, and good luck to you." The line went dead in O'Herlihy's hand.

"That Connor woman is behind this," O'Herlihy said as he hung up. "If it is the last thing I ever do, I will make her submit. She will pay that tax; the people of this state deserve a share of what she produces. She won't be able to stop working," O'Herlihy said as he paced up and down in his office. "She is a business robot; this is what she does. She is compelled to produce, and I am compelled to make sure that a share of what she produces is given to those who cannot produce anything."

"You really should get a Cat Scan," Mary Hawley sighed as she made notes. "There's something wrong with you."

"You shut up, Hawley, or I'll fire your ass."

"You won't have to," Hawley smiled as she handed over a copy of a document. "I put in for retirement two days ago. Bye," she smiled as she stood up.

"Good riddance, you old skunk," O'Herlihy smirked.

Fifteen minutes later Hawley, who had worked for Monarch as a teenager, was sitting in front of Christine.

"This is going to be fun; a lot of fun," she grinned. "Tell me what you need."

The Orion Motorcar Company

Lordship Boulevard

Stratford, Connecticut

October, 2008

"It's Jack Barden from Barden Steel on line two," Christine's secretary said.

"Hello, Jack; what can I do for you?" Christine said.

"Marry me," Jack laughed. "I'll pay anything."

"You don't have that much money."

"I will after I skin you alive in a business deal," Jack said.

"I don't need any price increases," Christine said. "I have enough problems as it is."

"So I hear. I got a rather strange call from Mercedes North America. They want to order a huge amount of steel."

"For what? They have one lousy plant in West Virginia. The rest of their crap is produced in the Fatherland."

"Police cars for the State of Connecticut," Jack said. "I'm tempted to make the deal. Unless, well, you know."

"Me naked on your conference table is not an option," Christine said.

"Buying my entire production run for the year is," Jack said. "I can't sell the Germans what I don't have."

"Only if I can order it delivered here as needed. I don't have any place to store that much steel. You could just tell them no, couldn't you?"

"Of course, but squeezing you is more fun."

"Don't get your hopes up," Christine laughed. "The only thing I have that you can squeeze is my checkbook. Is this going to work?" Christine said. "They can just go someplace else."

"Not if I make a few calls, they can't," Jack said. "I'm three hours away. Everybody else who could fill an order like that is days away. That adds a lot of cost to the order. Besides, I'll use my inestimable charm to tell them not to sell them any steel or you'll appear in their office some day on your broom."

"Then make those calls. And forget about me naked on your conference table."

"A man can dream, can't he? How about a picture of you in the shower?"

"Bye, Jack," Christine said, and hung up.

"Who's next?" Christine's secretary said.

"How do you stop the engine of the world?" Christine smiled. "You run it out of gas."

Office of the Governor

State Capitol

Hartford, Connecticut

October, 2008

"What do you mean we can't buy any gas?" O'Herlihy screeched.

"Our credit has been downgraded so badly nobody will deal with us," O'Herlihy's new secretary smiled as she let her skirt ride up. She bobbed her foot up and down, her red high heel perched on her toes. "I'll deal with you," she grinned. "For cash, of course."

"Never mind that," O'Herlihy snapped. "I have too many problems right now."

"Pussy cures everything," the girl said as she adjusted her nylons.

"Go type some letters. I have to get ready for my call to the President."

"President of what?" the girl laughed. "Texaco?"

"The President of the United States," O'Herlihy said.

"That should be fun," the girl snickered as she got up. "The halt leading the blind. You ever talk to him?"

"No. Why do you ask?"

"The Senator I used to fuck I mean work for used to talk to him all the time. Dude is way out there," she smiled, twirling her finger next to her temple. "Good luck."

That afternoon, the call came though.

"Hello, Mr. President," O'Herlihy said cheerfully.

"Am I still the President?" G.W. said.

"Yes you are," O'Herlihy said. "I could use some help with gasoline."

"Y'all can buy that at the Mobil Station down the road from here," G.W. grinned. "Good price, too. I fill up the limo there all the time. Don't even have to pay for it."

"Uh, that's nice. My problem is a bit different. A local car builder has convinced the major distributors not to sell the state any gasoline."

"Major Distributor? Is that Army? I can have a Colonel call him. A Colonel is better than a Major, right?"

"Yes, Mr. President, but I'm not talking about the military. Major means big. They won't sell the state any gasoline. I need gasoline for our police department."

"Well now; did y'all pay the bill? One time I forgot and Barbara couldn't get no gas for her Pinto. Raised hell about that, she did. Wouldn't sleep with me no more after that."

"You slept with ….. never mind," O'Herlihy said. "Can you help me? The government has reserves."

"I was in the Reserves," G.W. beamed. "Air Force, I think. You want to join up?"

"No, I don't. I need gas."

"Eat baked beans," G.W. said. "Friend's is the worst. Them things will give you gas you will not believe. Y'all can ask Barbara; she'll tell you. Kicked me out of bed, she did."

"You slept with your mother?" O'Herlihy exclaimed.

"Barbara is my mother?" G.W. exclaimed. "I never did figure out why she didn't want to do the wild thing with me. That other gal Laura did a time or two, but she said my feet smelled bad and she moved into the garage. Go figure."

"I really need your help, Mr. President. I need gasoline."

"Oh. Talk to my Energy Czar." The phone clicked, and a recording of Donald Duck began playing.

"Good grief," O'Herlihy sighed as he hung up. "We are all doomed."

Ten minutes later, his secretary sashayed in. "No food," she giggled.

"Huh? What do you mean, no food?" O'Herlihy said.

"The food you buy for all the state cafeterias, the prisons, the National Guard, and the nut houses. You do know what food is, don't you? Well, your contract got cut off by ShopMart. They said your credit sucks and you stiffed them on last month's bill."

"We did no such thing!" O'Herlihy roared, slamming his fist on the desk. "We send checks whether we have money or not!"

"Well, they said they didn't get one. If my paycheck don't clear, I'm out of here. Bye," she smiled as she went back to her desk.

"No," O'Herlihy cried as he put his head in his hands. "It's her; I know it is."

Office of Bob Purcell

Connecticut National Bank

Hartford, Connecticut

October, 2008

"I don't know if this is even legal," Purcell said as Carla sat down across from him and put her feet up on her desk. "Good grief; where's your underwear?" he whispered.

"Home in the drawer where it belongs," Carla smiled. "I like to feel the breeze between my knees. What do you mean, it ain't legal?"

"The state has overdraft privileges."

"Cancel 'em," Carla said as she adjusted her nylons. "Or you will lose squirrel privileges, handsome."

"I can't do that; the squirrel thing, I mean."

"Why not? Your dick broke or something?"

"No. I'm married."

"Same difference," Carla muttered. "Okay, how about a cash bribe, then? I got to get this done. My friend Christine wants it done, and what Christine wants, Christine gets. Want a new Orion?" she grinned.

"Well, my wife could use a new car," Purcell said. "But I can't afford one of her cars."

"You are a damn bank president, and y'all make shit money? You expect me to believe that? Besides, she will finance it for you. If you happen to miss a payment, like all 48 of 'em, I guarantee you will not have a problem."

"Are you sure? This could get me fired."

"Damn job ain't worth a shit anyway," Carla sighed. "Look, married man, you pass on me and a new car, you got to go for a cat scan because you got some serious brain damage. Take the damn car, already. Here's the finance contract and the title."

"Well, as long as it's legal. What excuse can I use to cancel their overdraft privileges?"

"How about they ain't got no money? That usually works, don't it?"

"Overdraft privileges are a form of credit. The state eventually pays us."

"Wait," Carla grinned. "Governor Fuckface is gonna be giving blowjobs in the bus station for a dollar a shot when we get through with his ass. You ain't likely to get paid; nobody else is," she shrugged. "They burned ShopMart, so Henry cut 'em off. Me sittin' on his face had nothin' to do with it, neither."

"What did O'Herlihy do to deserve this?" Purcell laughed.

"He pissed off the wrong person. Boy got to be taught a lesson."

The Orion Motorcar Company

Lordship Boulevard

Stratford, Connecticut

October, 2008

"Let's see how we can torture O'Herlihy today," Christine smiled as she sat down at her desk.

"Snow plow trucks," Mary Hawley said. "The state's are worn out, and winter is coming."

"Who does he buy them from?" Christine said.

"International Harvester. This could tie up the whole state, you know. First time it snows and those junkers we have start to break down, people will be stuck in their houses."

"Good," Christine said. "That will teach them to vote for a socialist. One of the best ways to fix a politician is to turn the voters against him."

Christine had her secretary get the President of International Harvester on the line.

"Oh, hello, Christine; how are you?" Mike Pompanelli said.

"Do I know you?" Christine said curiously.

"I was head of project development for your father before I came here. I met you several times."

"Oh, now I remember you! My word, what a small world. Can I get a favor?"

"Sure; name it. We Monarch alumni have to stick together."

"Well, our wonderful governor here in Connecticut is trying to squeeze successful businesses with some scheme to tax us into oblivion. I squeezed back, and would like to squeeze harder. He needs new snow plow trucks, and he buys them from you."

"Gee, that's too bad; I just looked outside, and we don't seem to have any. Also, other orders have to be filled first. I guess he's out of luck. Hey; my kid is going off to college. She could use something good to drive."

"You learned how to negotiate when you worked for my father, didn't you," Christine laughed. "My kind of extortionist. I'll have a new Orion SUV in your driveway by sundown. The lease contract will be mailed to you. I think a dollar a year would be about right."

"Works for me," Mike said.

"Thanks, Mike. Nice talking to you."

Residence of Caitlyn Meadows

87 West Reitter St.

Stratford, Connecticut

October, 2008

The man ambled up to Caitlyn's front door; he knew she wasn't home, because her car wasn't in the driveway. He looked around, then put an envelope containing $50,000.00 in cash between the screen door and the house door. He then walked back to his car, his hands in his pockets. Had Caitlyn seen him, she would have immediately thought of Charles Bronson's character Paul Kersey; he bore a strong resemblance to the famous actor. He got into a nondescript car and headed for the Orion Motorcar Company.

The Orion Motorcar Company

Lordship Boulevard

Stratford, Connecticut

October, 2008

"There's a man here to see you," Christine's secretary said. "I've never seen him before."

"What's his name?"

"Paul Smith."

"Oh, sure. Tell him to leave."

"He's ….different. Dangerous looking, but nice in a way I find hard to describe. He reminds me of you."

"All right," Christine sighed. "Put him through the metal detector and send him in." She unlocked the desk drawer that held her .45 and slid it open. The man came in and sat down.

"I'm Paul Smith," he smiled. "You must be Christine Connor."

"I am," Christine said. "You don't have an appointment."

"I never do," Smith said. He had a serious, deadly look about him, but in a good way.

"What's your real name?" Christine said. "And why were you carrying a gun?"

"Why do you have one in that desk drawer you opened before I came in?" Smith said.

"You first," Christine said.

"The world is a dangerous place; you never know when you might have to protect yourself."

Christine looked at Smith for a long time. "You're him, aren't you. The mystery man."

"Some call me that," Smith said. "Although what I do isn't all that mysterious."

"Exactly what is it that you do?" Christine said.

"I help people. Do you need help? I think you do."

"What kind of help?"

"Well, certainly not financial," Smith said as he looked around. "I'm not here to give you money, nor will I take any from you. I never accept payment for my help."

"And if I say I don't need any help?"

"Then I will leave you to your own devices."

"I'm not used to strangers showing up here offering help. It could be a trick. I have a lot of enemies."

"I know," Smith said. "People like us always do. What counts is how you deal with them, not how they deal with you. The antics of a thug are, shall we say, predictable and static. The way regular people react is not. I knew a

115

man a long time ago," Smith said, looking away. "He was a very ordinary man. His wife got caught in the middle of a stickup at a department store, and they killed her. He completely lost his mind; he found out who the two men were, and he went looking for them. He killed them both with point blank shotgun blasts to the face. Then he went home and shot himself. That's what I mean when I say you never know how somebody will react to bad people."

"And how should I react to politicians who think I should be used as one of the major food groups?"

Smith made a gun out of his thumb and first finger, and winked at Christine.

"I do not use violence unless I am physically attacked."

"And what's the difference between being physically attacked and financially attacked? Physical wounds heal. Financial ones rarely do."

"You've been watching too many movies, Mr. Smith. I am dealing with the state government, not a schoolyard bully."

"Is there really any difference? Both seek to accomplish the same thing, only by different means. Both respond very well to my type of solution."

"What are you going to do, shoot the Governor? Guess who'd be the prime suspect; me. Murder for hire carries a long prison sentence."

"No, I do not intend to shoot the Governor. Not today, anyway."

"That's all people like you know how to do, is kill."

"There are three different forms of death; physical, mental, and spiritual. Nobody recovers from any of them."

"You must have a lot of money if you run around the country saving the world."

"I have adequate means; what good is money in the long run if you never use it to do good?"

"Don't start the altruistic crap with me," Christine said. "I've heard that garbage all my life. I earned what money I have, and I will do with it as I please."

"I'm speaking about myself, not you."

"That's your choice, not mine. You can give away every dime you have for all I care."

"Like the old saying goes, you can't take it with you," Smith smiled.

"You haven't seen my coffin," Christine smirked. "I may just do exactly that."

"You have no one to leave this fabulous business and all your money to?"

"I might," Christine shrugged. "What do you care? You want to be in my will?"

"No, I want to make sure you're able to leave one. The Governor is not as meek as you think."

"I don't need a bodyguard," Christine said. "Or a hit man."

"I'm not a hit man."

"No? What do you call it, then? Retribution? Revenge? This is a nation of laws."

"It is, and it is designed to do justice, but it is ultimately backed by force. When the police come for you, they have guns. I dispense justice with a gun, too; I just cut out the middle man."

"Then you promote anarchy."

"Anarchy is very useful at times; what we did in 1776 was considered anarchy by England. Where would we be today had the founding fathers followed English law?"

"I'd be in London competing against Rolls-Royce," Christine said. "Where would you be?"

"Dead," Smith smiled. "I refuse to live where there is no freedom. I hear you love your life; is that true?"

"Yes, it is."

"The line between love and hate is so thin it is almost indistinguishable. If you lose this fight, what will you love then? You can always call me if you change your mind."

"You have a telephone?" Christine smirked.

"Sure," Smith smiled. "Doesn't everybody?" He put a business card on the desk and left. Christine took out a pair of tweezers, put the card in a plastic bag, and called Harper. She arrived fifteen minutes later.

"What's up?" she said.

"I want you to find out who this man is," Christine said, handing over the plastic bag.

"Why? Did he threaten you or something?" Harper said.

"No, he did not. He offered to help me."

"Nothing illegal about that," Harper shrugged. "What did he look like?"

"Charles Bronson's twin brother."

"Oh, him. I've heard about him. He gives away money to crime victims, and supposedly kills perpetrators."

"Remind you of anybody?" Christine smirked. "Like your partner, perhaps?"

"You want me to help you?" Harper said.

"Yes."

"Then lay off Carla." She thought for a minute, then tossed the bag onto Christine's desk. "This isn't a police matter," she said. "And I don't work for you. Find out who he is all by your lonesome." She got up and headed for the door.

"Wait," Christine said "He intimated that he would kill people; perhaps the Governor."

"That's nice," Harper smirked. "I'll put him in for a medal."

"I would be a suspect, considering I am having a financial war with the state."

"You should stick to building cars," Harper said, "because you don't know shit about the law. In order to be charged with murder or murder for hire, one of you has to be apprehended by the police, and testify against the other. An exchange of money has to be promised or have taken place. From what I've heard about this dude, nobody will ever catch him. And you certainly don't fit the bill for a hit girl."

"Nobody can catch him? Not even the vaunted Stratford Police?" Christine said.

"Nope. I wouldn't even try; I'm not that fond of politicians. Besides, we don't have jurisdiction in Hartford, or wherever the chooch Governor lives. If your pal surfaces again, tell him not to shoot the bastard in Stratford."

"You don't seem too concerned that a murderer came to my office."

"I'm not," Harper said. "He apparently broke no laws. Let's get something straight, Chrissy; I don't like you. I never have. I don't know what hold you have on Carla, but you had better knock it off. If you soften her up and make her ineffective as a cop you'll have to deal with me, and you won't like that one fucking little bit."

"What did I ever do to you?" Christine laughed.

"It's your holier-than-thou attitude. You think you're better than us common folks, but we're the first ones you run to when you get yourself into a jam."

"I am capable of handling the Governor. I just thought you might want to know this man is in your town."

"How the hell do you know where he is?" Harper laughed. "Besides; until he breaks a law, he can stay anywhere he likes. He's no danger to you, is he?"

"No, he is not. He seems very nice."

"Good. Take him out to dinner and give him a blowjob."

"You are a crude, insufferable person who has no class."

"And that's one of my better qualities," Harper said. "I suggest you avoid doing anything that would result in me showing you some of the bad ones."

"I think that's all you have, is bad ones."

"I don't give two shits what you think. You want to tangle assholes with me? Bring your lunch."

"I have no desire to have a confrontation with the police. I will talk to Carla about this. She is your boss, you know."

"Go ahead," Harper smirked. "You don't know her as well as you think you do. Cross Carla and she'll stuff your corpse into a garbage dumpster someplace, and they'll never see you again."

"How charming, to know our police department is staffed by murderers."

"You don't like the way we do our job? Fucking move, and take your car plant with you. Nobody asked you to come here."

"This is a free country."

"This is my country," Harper nodded. "Twenty four hours a day. You remember that next time you feel like shooting off your big mouth because I, unlike Carla, will not hesitate to close it for you."

"Just what I would expect from you; violence."

"Then you won't be disappointed when I break your jaw for you. I'm leaving. If that dude threatens you, we'll go have a talk with him."

"How? You don't know where he is."

"We can find him if we need to," Harper smirked. "Bet on it."

Collici's Italian Pavilion Restaurant

Grand Street

Bridgeport, Connecticut

October, 2008

"Happy dance," Tony Collici grinned when he saw Carla, Harper, and Clodagh come in. "Although youse caused a lot of trouble for me last time youse was here. Youse whack Don Carmine D'Allessio?"

"I don't know," Harper shrugged. "I whacked a lot of mob dudes; you fat dummies all look alike."

"He took a dive out the window at Bridgeport Hospital," Tony said.

"Oh, really? Must have broken up with his gay lover."

"Get us a table, fat boy," Carla said. "I am not in a good mood. It be Tomater Sauce Tuesday real soon."

"When was youse ever in a good mood?" Tony said.

"Fuck youse," Carla grinned. "How you like that, boy?"

"What's youse?" Clodagh said.

"Means you, only maybe there's more than one. It's an Italian thing. Wese means me but there's more than one. Sometimes, anyway. I ain't sure about this. There ain't no Guinea dictionary," Tony said.

"Hey!" Carla said, waving at Tony. "Y'all understand italiano morto?"

"Mio Dio," Tony gasped, crossing himself. "Never say that to an Italian businessman."

"Monkey business," Carla muttered. "Make with the menus, dude. This ain't a social call."

A waiter appeared. "Yo, I'm like Jimmy. Youse want menus?"

"No, we'll just read your mind," Harper smiled. "Shouldn't take too long."

"Youse is like funny," Jimmy said.

"Never mind the menus," Carla sighed. "Chicken Parm, Lasagna, Spaghetti and Meatballs, Antipasto, bread, six pizzas, and red wine. And blackberry brandy. Lots of it."

"Lots of what?" Jimmy said.

"Everything, dumbass," Carla said. "You related to Andrew Dice Clay?"

"Little Miss Muffet sat on her tuffet," Jimmy grinned, and went to put in the order.

"Look," Harper whispered as Paul Smith came in and was shown to a table in the back corner. "That's the dude Christine told me about."

"Well now; maybe I will have me a talk with him," Carla said. She went over to Smith's table and showed her badge. "Chief Larsen. You are Paul Smith, correct?"

"Yes I am," Smith smiled. "Sit down. Would you like something to eat?"

"I got food ordered yonder."

"Yonder? You aren't from around here, are you."

"I am from Kansas, lived in Corn-necticut since 1994. Where you from?"

"I was born in California. I have lived all over the country; mostly hotels. I have no permanent address."

"How convenient. Christine Connor is my friend. What do you want with her?"

"Nothing. I offered her some help, and she declined. It was a rather short conversation."

"What kind of help?"

"I don't know. She never got as far as telling me about her issue; some sort of government problem from what I hear. That's usually above my pay grade."

"I've heard all about your pay grade," Carla said as she helped herself to some of Smith's wine. "Paul Smith, huh? You look Slavic, and you are a dead ringer for that actor who liked to shoot people on the subway. I bet that ain't your real name."

"It is if I say so," Smith said.

"What was it before you changed it?"

"Who says I changed it?" Smith said.

"Talkin' to you is like me talkin' to my Commish. No real answers."

"What do you want of me?"

"Well, first of all I would like to know if you got a permit for that gun you were packing in Christine's office."

"Oh, that. It was a water pistol," Smith grinned.

"This is total bullshit," Carla sighed. "You think I ain't never been through shit like this with a suspect?"

"Now I'm a suspect? For offering Miss Connor some help? That's hardly a crime."

"I know what you do," Carla said. "Now me bein' who I am, I cannot tell you I disapprove of anybody who puts bad guys away. That aside, I enforce the law in Stratford. That includes takin' care of folks like you if they step out of line. You do anything illegal in my town, and you will pay a dear price."

"I save lives and protect the public," Smith said as he poured more wine for both of them. "Just like you. The fact that I do not carry a badge doesn't change that one bit in my mind."

"Makes it different in court," Carla said. "Makes y'all a vigilante. That is illegal."

"Only if I get caught and can't claim self defense," Smith said.

"All right, let's cut the shit," Carla sighed. "Just behave yourself in Stratford, or else. I got enough work as it is without chasin' your ass around."

"Need any help?" Smith smiled.

"Fuckin' smartass," Carla said, shaking her head. "You remember what I said."

Nevis International Bank & Trust

Nevis International Bank & Trust Center

October, 2008

"You!" Sir Frederick Whittington exclaimed. "What are you doing here again? You beat me up last December."

"Indeed I did," Harper said. "A little ass kicking is good for the soul. You don't look any worse for wear. Still got your job though, just like I told you."

"What do you want? The stockholders were very suspicious about that story I told them. They found it hard to believe that strangers could come into my office and force me to make transfers. If I was not a member of the Royal Family, I would have been fired."

"You're a royal pain in the ass is what you are," Harper said.

"Start your computer, Jack," Clodagh said. "We're gonna play switcheroo."

"Who is the victim now?"

"Dead drug dealer," Harper said, wandering around behind Whittington.

"How did he die?" Whittington said nervously.

"You could say he lost his head," Harper shrugged. "He won't complain. And if you do, you can join him. We don't want to do that; we want you to stay here and help us when some other bastard stashes his ill gotten gains in your bank. Now type, motherfucker. Bartram Edwards."

Whittington brought Edwards' account up on the screen.

"Whoa," Harper said. "This dude had some serious cash. A hundred and fourteen billion? You guys must pay some serious interest. I have forty dollars; can I invest it here?"

"You have eight million from your last visit as I recall; a Mr. Stanton donated to your family trust."

"Oh, that. He turned out to be not guilty, so we gave it back to him. Transfer that money to my trust. We don't have all day."

"A transfer of this magnitude requires approval by the board."

"The only magnitude you're going to get is a .357 magnitude in the head. You make that transfer, or I will. You'll never see me do it though, because you'll be dead. And why does it need approval?"

"Because you claim the man is dead. We must verify that before we uh, dispose of the funds. You know; check for legal heirs."

"The fucking guy was a crooked congressman dope dealer. He never did anything legal in his life, heirs or otherwise. You think a congressman makes that kind of money? You can also look up his case on the docket at

Bridgeport Superior Court. He was convicted on all accounts. He had his head blown off by persons unknown. You can go online and see the news story. Happened at Osborn Correctional in Somers, Connecticut. That money is going to be turned over to the U.S. Treasury. Most of it, anyway," she grinned. "And don't pull any shit after we leave, or I will come back. You know what that means, don't you?"

"I assume it means my immediate demise," Whittington said.

"Oh, you'll demise all right, but it won't be immediate. It'll be nice and slow. I think the record for us torturing somebody is three days. Care to challenge that?"

"No, I do not. I uh, could use some remuneration myself."

"Re what? That better not be something dirty," Harper said.

"Compensation," Whittington said. "A piece of the action, as you Americans say. After all, I don't have to do this."

"Yes you do. So you're a crook after all," Harper sighed. "I thought so. How much?"

"A million pounds Sterling," Whittington said. "Surely you can spare that."

"Okay, take it. And don't call me Shirley," Harper grinned. "I always wanted to say that to somebody."

Harper stood behind Whittington with her cell phone and filmed him transferring the money to himself. She showed him the little movie.

"You cross us and I'll send this to your boss," she nodded. "That's what we Americans call Talk-O El Fuck-O."

"Cute," Whittington said as he transferred the rest of the money to Harper's "Boone Family Trust." She then had him wire all of it to Carla's bank in Kansas.

"Remember Carla?" Harper smiled.

"Who could forget her," Whittington said. "Little Devil that she is."

"She owns that bank you just sent that money to. You screw us, and you are royally dead. She will bury you alive."

"You have my assurance that I will keep your confidence. My position with the Royal Family would be destroyed if word of this was to be disclosed. My lands and titles would be revoked, and my family would be expelled."

"Okay, Lord Asswipe," Clodagh said. "We get the picture. We just want to make sure we have something on you. That's called leverage. Carla learned that from Bill Clinton."

"Another charming chap," Whittington smirked. "Are we done?"

"Yeah," Harper shrugged. "Just don't pull any shit, okay? If you do, you'll be done."

The Orion Motorcar Company

Lordship Boulevard

Stratford, Connecticut

October, 2008

"That much, huh?" Carla grinned as she pulled into the Orion parking lot. "And it's in my bank?"

"Yes, and don't get any ideas about giving it all away. Or giving it to the government," Harper said. "It wasn't taken from them, so they have no claim on it. Especially since nobody ever told them how much Bartram had."

"There's a dude on the roof with a rifle," Carla grinned. "Chrissy must have got her a death threat. Bet she about peed her britches if she did."

"That's her idea of security? Some asshole with a rifle in plain sight on the roof? Maybe we should teach her something about security."

"I'm down for that," Carla nodded as they got out.

"You're down for a lot of things," Harper muttered. The man peered down at them and got on his radio.

Ten minutes later, Carla and Harper came into Christine's office. They had the guard on a hand truck; he was duct taped hand and foot, and had his mouth taped as well. They dumped the guard on the floor, sat down, and grinned at Christine.

"Y'all got shit security," Carla said. "Best hire somebody who knows what the hell he's doing."

"I see," Christine said. "Release him." Carla cut the tape loose, and the guard stood up.

"I could have shot you, you know," he nodded.

"Sure; and I can win Virgin of the year," Carla said. "You ever point a rifle at me, and you will die."

"You are relieved of your duties, Malcolm," Christine said. "Permanently. Go back to your agency and be glad these two let you."

"How did you do that?" Christine said after Malcolm had gone. "He was in the Marines."

"Marines don't teach cop work," Carla said. "What for you got some dude on the roof with a rifle?"

"The Governor is very displeased with me," Christine said. "I don't take chances."

"Dude on the roof with a rifle ain't gonna save you; a good hitter will get you when you leave the building."

"I hardly ever leave. I live upstairs."

"You're in way over your head," Carla said. "You build cars; you don't know shit about killers."

"Then who does, besides you? The state is almost bankrupt because of what I did."

"Tough titty," Harper smirked. "You sowed it; now reap it. Can't take a little push back from a cheap politician?"

"Push back is one thing; murder is another."

"Well, you started it. If you can't finish it, that's your mistake. The police can't help you."

"Can't, or won't?" Christine said.

"Really isn't much difference, is there?" Harper said. "If that panty wearing asshole in Hartford has you killed in Stratford, we'll investigate. Other than that, handle your own problems. We aren't a bodyguard service."

"That's reassuring," Christine said.

"Harpo is right," Carla said. "Y'all started a fight you are not equipped to finish. Anybody threaten you?"

"Somebody left a brochure in my car. It's from a funeral parlor."

"You touch it?" Harper said.

"No. It's still there."

"Fetch," Harper grinned. She took a pair of surgical gloves and an evidence bag out of her purse. "I thought you parked inside."

"I do," Christine said.

"That should tell you something," Harper said as Christine headed for the door. "This is bullshit," Harper said to Carla. "She insults me every time I see her, then she wants us to help her."

"Run the brochure for prints," Carla sighed.

"Probably a funeral director doing some advertising," Harper grumbled.

"In a locked garage?"

"Shit, I could get into her garage or anybody else's in three minutes or less."

"Morticians ain't the kind of people that pick locks."

"All right, I'll have Clo-dog run it for prints. Chrissy should stop fucking with people. She isn't qualified."

"I'll make that clear to her." Christine came back; Harper took the evidence bag and left without a word.

"She doesn't like me," Christine said.

"You blame her?" Carla said.

"I guess not. I am a bit of a snippy tyrant at times. I'm sorry."

"You're telling the wrong person."

"I'm not apologizing to her," Christine huffed. "Why should I?"

"No reason I can think of," Carla shrugged. "Just keep bein' good old Christine and piss everybody off. And you best knock off the bullshit with the state. Messing with politicians is above your pay grade."

"I will not be used for their personal ATM machine," Christine said. "Would you put up with that?"

"Nope. Me, I'd just kill the son of a bitch and leave his ass on the highway bare ass naked. Shit like that sends a real clear message."

"I cannot do that," Christine said.

"Tell me about it," Carla said. "I will fix this for you, but it's the last time."

Stratford Police Department

900 Longbrook Ave.

Stratford, Connecticut

October, 2008

"Bingo," Clodagh said as she tossed a file onto Harper's desk. "Prints came back to Loren Lilly. High line pro hitter with about forty arrests to his credit; no.... corn-victions," she grinned at Carla.

Harper tossed the file to Carla. "Here, Mattress Millie; Chrissy is your project, not mine."

"Y'all got a real bad attitude about the gal," Carla said.

"Fuck her. And you too, if you don't like it."

"Whoa! You gonna take that from her, Kemosabe?" Clodagh said.

"Fuck her and the horse she sucked off last night," Carla mused as she went through the file. "This asshole means business," she said. "He must like whackin' folks. I reckon it's time he were on the receivin' end."

"You're going to kill somebody for Little Miss Moneybags?" Harper said.

"Nah, it'll be self de-fense. Boys like that do not like bein' arrested," Carla grinned. "Then I figure to go have me a talk with the Governor and put an end to this. Fear not; I told Christine this is the last time."

"Sure it is," Harper said. "Until the next time. What is it with you two?"

"It ain't," Carla said. "We just talk about business and other shit occasionally. You got a problem with that?"

"She thinks Christine is turning you into a liberal weenie, and you'll suck at being a cop after that," Clodagh said.

"I can speak for myself," Harper said. "She's turning you into a liberal weenie, and you'll suck at being a cop after that."

"She got no corn-trol over me. I am that I am."

"And that's all that I am; I'm Popeye the Sailor Man..." Harper sang.

"Eat me, Olive Oyl," Carla grinned. "Hey, who was the dude that ate all the hamburgers?"

"Bill Clinton," Harper snickered.

"Wimpy," Clodagh said. "There was another dude in the cartoons called Poopdeck Pappy. I wonder if he took it in the ....."

"Stop," Carla said. "That is an image I can do without."

"Kind of like the Road Runner wearing a skirt," Harper grinned.

"Now you are out of line," Carla said. "I got a killer to kill I mean talk to. Who wants to go with me?"

"I'll go," Clodagh said. "Whiny Wanda ovadere might rat you out. I'll have Space Cadet find him."

Surf and Sand Motel

Cove Place

Lordship, Connecticut

October, 2008

"Asshole used his own credit card," Clodagh grinned. "He's almost as dumb as you."

"Ever been throwed out of a Fairlane at eighty miles an hour?" Carla said as they turned onto Cove Place.

"Nope. Besides, you're doing thirty miles an hour."

"Day ain't over yet. This place is kind of fancy; we got to take him out of here without nobody suspects nothing. What room number?"

"Seven. It faces the water."

"Parkin' lot is on the wrong side. We got to walk him out the front, which ain't good. Somebody might recognize me."

"Wear a wig, Kelly," Clodagh said. "A blonde one. Make sure it matches your hair color."

"I got to think about this," Carla said as she parked near the western edge of the lot.

"Oh, okay. I'll come back in a couple of days," Clodagh said. "You should be done by then."

"Okay, I got it. I got nurse's outfits in the trunk with surgical masks. Do not ask why, either. We will go in there and say we are from the free clinic, and the boy needs to be quarantined."

"This should be just fucking great," Clodagh sighed as she got out of the car. Five minutes later, they were standing in front of the front desk.

"Room 7," Carla said in a low voice. "Boy is infected bad with V.D. and we have to take him back to the clinic. We just got the results," she said, holding up a clip board. "It ain't good."

"I can't read that; it's too far away," the desk manager said.

"You aren't supposed to read it," Clodagh snapped. "It's confidential. You want this whole place to come down with Chronic obstructive hemostatic penis disease? It can be fatal, and it spreads faster than Nurse Ratchet here at a Hell's Angels picnic."

"Take him," the boy said, backing away. He tossed them the room key.

"What are you backing away from us for?" Clodagh said. "We don't have it; the guy in room 7 has it. You'd better burn everything in that room and have it disinfected, too."

They proceeded to room 7, guns drawn. Carla opened the door slowly; Lilly was in the kitchenette, his back to them. She snuck up behind him and brained him with a vase. They scooped his semi unconscious form off the floor and walked him out of the motel.

The Fall Family Farm

Route 22

Amenia, New York

October, 2008

"Did you fart, you bastard?" Clodagh shrieked as she covered her face and tried to open her window, which Carla had locked. "God, that stinks!"

"Supposed to," Carla grinned. "You and Harpie are always on my ass; thought you might like to see what I can do with it."

"I'm going to puke," Clodagh gagged. "Open the window or I'll heave in your lap."

"Damn sissy," Carla sighed as she lowered the window. "You'd think you never smelled shit before."

"You should be euthanized," Clodagh mumbled as she stuck her head out the window.

"Quit your damn complainin'," Carla said as she pulled onto the road leading to the farm. She got out and closed the gate behind her. They pulled up in front of the house and got out of the car.

"I think one of my lungs collapsed," Clodagh said as she started coughing.

"You'll live. He won't, though," Carla said, pointing at the trunk. "Go make us some pancakes. I got a hole to dig."

After they had eaten, Carla emitted a roaring belch and rubbed her stomach. "Excuse me," she grinned. "See that? I got manners. They ain't worth a shit, but I got 'em. Less go have us a talk with Leroy."

"It's Loren," Clodagh said.

"That's a girl's name, not a proper name for no killer."

"Well fucking sue the dude, okay? Who cares what his name is."

They pulled Lilly out of the trunk by the hair and dragged him over to the eight foot deep hole Carla had dug with the backhoe.

"What the hell are you doing?" he shrieked. "Who are you?"

"Death and Taxis," Carla grinned.

"It's …. never mind," Clodagh sighed. "What's the use."

Carla dumped Lilly by the hole and kicked him. "Y'all like leavin' funeral parlor magazines in Christine Connors' car, Mr. Hit Man? Should've left one in your own damn car."

"I don't know what you're talking about," Lilly said. "Let me go."

"Oh, like that's going to happen," Clodagh laughed. "You think we drove all the way up here 'to let you go?"

"I did nothing wrong. There must be a mistake," Lilly said.

"The mistake was you didn't wear gloves, asshole; you left your prints all over that brochure. We know who you are, Mr. Lilly," Clodagh said. "You've made quite a career out of killing people. Career over."

"Who ordered the hit?" Carla yawned.

"I told you, there must be a mistake."

"Talk, boy. I will not ask again." Carla took out a small propane torch, lit it, and unzipped Lilly's pants. "Four, three, two……"

"The Governor," Lilly babbled as the torch came closer to his groin.

"Good boy," Carla said. She kicked Lilly into the hole and went over to the backhoe.

"Noooooo!" Lilly screamed. "You can't!"

"Yes I can, and shut the hell up. Decent folks are tryin' to have lunch hereabouts, dipshit. They don't want to listen to you. Take your punishment like a man," Carla said. She started the backhoe and began pushing dirt into the hole. Lilly's screams were soon stifled as his mouth filled with dirt. When the little project was complete and the hole covered with leaves, Carla put the backhoe away and headed for the car.

"How long does it take to die like that?" Clodagh said as she got in.

"Dunno; I ain't never been buried alive," Carla said. "Couple hours, I reckon. These asshole criminals are startin' to piss me off, makin' me come up here all the damn time. Racing gas ain't cheap, you know."

"Buy a Volkswagen," Clodagh said.

"Trunk ain't big enough," Carla grinned.

"You gonna whack the Governor? That will bring major heat down on us."

"How? Ain't nobody gonna be able to prove diddly. We will have us an alibi. We will be at work in the station, gettin' caught up on paperwork."

"Then how are we going to make him …. you know?"

"We ain't," Carla grinned. "I still got Paul Smith's number. But I aim to talk to the boy first. Maybe he will see the error of his ways."

"Or a backhoe," Clodagh grinned.

Office of the Governor

State Capitol

Hartford, Connecticut

November, 2008

"There's a cop here to see you," the secretary said. "Girl from Stratford. Carla Larsen."

"Send her in." O'Herlihy stood up as Carla came in. "What can I do for you, Miss Larsen?" he said.

Carla made sure the door was locked, and sat down. She stared at O'Herlihy for a long minute.

"I got four words for y'all," Carla sighed. "Connor, cut the shit."

"Did she send you?" O'Herlihy said.

"Nope. She don't know I am here."

"What's this cut the shit stuff about?"

"You know what it's about. Do not shine me on; I am much too smart for you."

"I am the Governor of this state. You're just a cop."

"Oh, but I am much more than a cop. I am the Chief of Detectives in Stratford, an Assistant State's Attorney, an Assistant U.S. Attorney, and a deputized FBI Agent. I also got access to G.W. hisself and some military shit you would not believe. I can lock your crooked ass up or make it disappear if I am of a mind to."

"Sure you can. What's the point of your little visit? I have work to do."

"I see what kind of work you like to do," Carla smiled. She tossed a manila folder full of photos onto O'Herlihy's desk. He almost had a seizure when he saw them.

"Where did you …… never mind. These were not taken in a public place; you can't use them in court."

"Wasn't going to. You want to bang hookers, that's your business. For now, anyway," she grinned. "I got other plans for them pictures."

"You think you can blackmail me?" O'Herlihy laughed.

"Nope. Don't have to. You see, I had one of my detectives get all your financial records. That's some stash you got in that safe deposit box in Massachusetts. And don't get no ideas about cleanin' it out, neither. I already got a court order against the bank. You are not allowed to go into that branch, and the manager will do ten years if he lets you. That is called gathering evidence against a cheap fuckin' crook. That would be you."

"You fuck with me and you'll disappear, you lousy no good bitch. There won't be enough left of you to put in a shoe box."

"Really?" Carla smiled. "Who's gonna do it, your boy Loren Lilly? I had me a talk with him, and he agreed to go away and never come back."

"I don't believe you; you're bluffing."

Carla tossed the funeral brochure onto O'Herlihy's desk. "Look familiar? Boy put that in Christine Connor's car."

"I don't know anything about that."

"Lilly said otherwise. But enough about him; you want to tango with me? That will be the biggest mistake of your life, and the last one. All those records will go to the state and federal District Attorneys, and somebody's wife is gona get an envelope full of pictures to help her in her dee-vorce case. After all, that would be the right thing to do. You agree?" she grinned.

"Fuck you. Get out."

"I ain't done talkin' yet," Carla said as O'Herlihy reached for a drawer in his desk. "I do not advise trying to play quick draw with me," she nodded as she took out her Colt and pointed it at him. "Hands back on the desk, and they better be empty."

O'Herlihy complied. Carla got up and opened the drawer; there was a Beretta 92F inside.

"Y'all been watchin' too many Lethal Weapon movies," she said. She popped the clip, opened the office window, and threw the Beretta into the parking lot six stories below.

"Hey! That gun is perfectly legal!" O'Herlihy shouted.

"Good. When some spook picks it up and shoots somebody with it, you can take the heat. Now where was we? Oh, I know. You were gonna promise to leave Christine alone, and cancel that tax legislation."

"You're crazy."

"That I am. You want to find out what crazy looks like in your fuckin' bedroom at three AM? I got friends even crazier than me, and that is going some. You see, you do not seem to understand what you got yourself into here. I don't bluff, I don't talk a lot of shit, and I do not exaggerate. I just do things with no warning. My main mission in life is to get rid of crooks like you, by any means necessary. Legal, illegal, don't make no difference to me," she shrugged.

"And if I refuse?"

"That's your problem. Oh, and one more thing; resign."

"What?" O'Herlihy laughed. "No way."

"Okay," Carla shrugged. She got up and headed for the door. "You know, we got a saying in Stratford. Sometimes you just can't help yourself, and you pick on the wrong person. Say hello to the wrong person."

"Out," O'Herlihy said.

"Okay. Like they say at Burger King, have it your way."

Stratford Police Department

900 Longbrook Ave.

Stratford, Connecticut

November, 2008

"Did he go for it?" Clodagh said.

"Course not. Man is a total asshole. Thinks who he is."

"And?"

"And I just faxed them pictures and a tape of him threatenin' me to all the TV and radio networks in the state, and I sent a set to his wife Fedex with that deliver the fuckin' package yesterday option they got. Boy is gonna have some 'splainin' to do when he gets home tonight."

"He'll fucking kill you," Clodagh giggled.

"He'll try," Carla said. "I like a good challenge. I been up against politicians before. We retired a couple of Governors already; one more won't make nobody cry."

"And what's he get if he tries to put a hit on you?"

"Chalk outline," Carla said.

Residence of Governor Dan O'Herlihy

17 Still Road

West Hartford, Connecticut

November, 2008

"Bastard whore," O'Herlihy muttered as he headed for the front door at noon. He had cooked up what he thought was a good bullshit story to tell his wife Connie, who was waiting for him inside in a little alcove next to the door. "Dead is what that cop is going to get," he fumed as he put the key in the lock.

He stepped inside and failed to notice the clear plastic on the floor; "Connie? Come down here. I have something to discuss with you."

Connie stepped out of the alcove, a gigantic cast iron frying pan in her hands. She executed a swing that would make Babe Ruth jealous, and bonged O'Herlihy square in the forehead. He rocketed backwards into the door frame, staggered forward, and started to go down. When he was collapsing onto his knees, Connie slammed him on top of the head as hard as she could. O'Herlihy crashed to the floor, foaming at the mouth. He twitched violently for a few seconds, emitted a high pitched squeak, and stopped moving.

"Asshole," Connie muttered. She put the frying pan in the dishwasher and turned it on. Their Goldendoodle came over, sniffed O'Herlihy's corpse, and peed on it. "Good boy," Connie giggled.

She dragged her dead husband's body into the back yard a hundred yards from the house and wedged it between two big boulders near some trees. She soaked O'Herlihy in gasoline and lit him up. The nearest house was a quarter of a mile away, and the wind was just right; it carried the awful stench off to the north towards Auerfarm State Park Scenic Reserve. She added kerosene to the fire every half hour; by dinnertime, there was nothing left of O'Herlihy but a pile of ashes and some charred bones. She waited until the bones cooled off, put them in a plastic lawn bag, and put the bag in the trunk of her car. O'Herlihy's final resting place would be the trunk of a junk Chevy in a salvage yard her brother owned; within 48 hours he would be in an Indiana steel mill where the Chevy would be melted down.

The next morning, her neighbor Dawn came over.

"What was that smell yesterday?" she said. "It smelled like burning flesh."

"It was Dan," Connie grinned. "He forgot to clean the barbecue. Spontaneous combustion."

"Oh; where is the creep?" Dawn said.

"Business trip. Indiana," Connie snorted. "I have a funny feeling he won't be coming back."

"Good," Dawn said. "I never liked him anyway."

"Makes two of us," Connie said. "Screw him; he probably ran off with some hooker. Look," she said, handing Dawn the lurid photos Fedex had delivered the prior day. "I'm on all the accounts, and the house is in my name. Who needs him. He'll be declared legally dead in a few weeks, and I can collect his pension."

"Indiana, huh?" Dawn grinned. "I bet he'll like it there."

"Too bad he won't get to see the scenery," Connie said.

Stratford Police Department

900 Longbrook Ave.

Stratford, Connecticut

November, 2008

"The Governor ain't been to work in two weeks," Carla grinned. "My guess is his old lady done for his ass. She was on the news, all teary eyed. Bet she had an onion in her pocket."

"Lot of that going around these days," Clodagh said. "Fathers fucking anything with a pulse, then turning up dead seems to be the new normal."

"I like the old normal," Carla said.

"You aren't normal," Clodagh snickered.

"Guess nobody is these days. All's well that ends with a bullet, as they say. The legislature dropped that new tax bill after Danny Boy disappeared. Christine is in the clear, and I don't even have to call Paul Smith."

"Tell Christine to knock it off. Harper is getting pissed off."

"Too damn bad. Better pissed off than pissed on," Carla grinned. "Harper got her an attitude. Thinks she can call the shots hereabouts."

"She's your best friend," Clodagh said. "Doesn't that count for something?"

"Not when it comes to her tellin' me what to do, it don't. I took her in when her Ma couldn't take no more of her bullshit, and I trained her to be a cop. She got a big fuckin' mouth, and I do not abide by that. On the other hand, she don't tolerate my big mouth neither. We have rassled in the ring four times as I recall, and may do so again if I am of a mind to kick her ass some more."

"I don't get it."

"Maybe you ain't supposed to get it."

"Maybe not. Oh, I forgot; Vito said a patrolman name of Dale McGraw wants to talk to you."

"Quick Draw? What's he want?"

"He killed a perp."

'Oh; he want a medal or something?"

"No; he's upset. He never shot anybody before."

"Boy been on the job eight years and he never capped anybody off. That's why he never made Detective."

"Is it a requirement that you kill people to be on the squad?" Clodagh said.

"No, but it is a requirement that you be willing and able to if the need arises, without cryin' like a little girl about it later. I will talk to the boy tomorrow."

Stratford Police Department

900 Longbrook Ave.

Stratford, Connecticut

November, 2008

"Have a seat, Quick Draw," Carla said.

"Don't call me that," McGraw said.

"Seems y'all forgot who got stars on their collar hereabouts," Carla said. "I will call you any damn thing I want. Who did you waste?"

"A drug dealer name of Sammy Williams, Jr."

"Good old Sammy; I knew he'd get fixed eventually. What happened?"

"I saw him make a sale. I went to arrest him, and he pulled a nine millimeter on me."

"You outdraw the boy?"

"I already had my service weapon out."

Carla peered down at McGraw's lap. "You did?" she grinned. "You figure to give him the high hard one?"

"The other weapon," McGraw sighed.

"We call it a gun, not a service weapon. You read the po-lice manual at night or somethin'?" Carla said as she stuffed a plug of Virginia twist into her cheek.

"Are you actually going to chew that?" McGraw exclaimed.

"Hell yeah," Carla said. "I stuck it in my mouth, didn't I? The tobaccy, that is. Not somebody's service weapon. Ain't nobody else gonna chew it for me. You want some?"

"No. That's disgusting."

"You should see it when it comes back out. Now, why are you all wound up about terminatin' a no good bastard drug dealer who drew down on you? That don't make no sense."

"I never killed anybody before. What about you? How did you react your first time?"

"Yelled stick it in harder," Carla grinned. "Oh, you mean wastin' somebody. I ferget, mostly. I were only seven years old at the time. Didn't really bother me, as I recall."

"Seven? Are you serious? What the hell were you doing killing people at that age?"

"Gettin' even with a boy in the orphanage who thought leavin' his fingerprints on my ass were a good idea. Billy Ray Stafford was his name. Me and another gal tortured him to death."

"I can see why you don't care about how I feel."

"Look, McGraw; I ain't a shrink and I ain't gonna waste a lot of time on this. If you cannot recover in short order when you do your duty, go get a different job."

"Is that it? You tell me I have to like killing people to be a cop?"

"I did not say that. You ain't listening. What if some other asshole runnin' buddy of Sammy's came along ten minutes later and decided to get some payback on your ass? If you was standin' there like Shirley Temple cryin' in your beer, you would be a prime target and would be in the morgue today. You been on the job long enough to know how it works; ain't a cop alive ain't been faced with that decision. You done the right thing; had you not, your name could be on a slab of granite by the end of the week."

"There are patrolmen here who have over twenty years service and never drew their weapon."

"Yeah, I know. They sleep behind the ShopMart and don't take radio calls when they should. I got about six of 'em I intend to have retire real soon. Ever ask yourself why some guys never move up the ladder? Twenty fuckin' years on the job and they're still in a radio car? They are fundamental cowards who just want to collect a pension, and they got no intention of riskin' their hide in the meantime. Boys like that never make Detective."

"Some people are happy in a radio car," McGraw shrugged. "Tracy O'Neil and her cousin Margo love patrol."

"Yeah, but they got big rank. They do patrol now and then because they want to, not because they have to."

"So I can cram all the police courses I want, but I'll never make Detective; is that what you're telling me?"

"You do a happy dance next time you shoot some asshole drug dealer and we will discuss your future in this department."

"I heard all about you; you like killing people, don't you. There are a lot of rumors about you taking things into your own hands."

"They ain't rumors," Carla said. "And never you mind what I do. Only thing you ever took into your own hands is your dick. I do not abide a crybaby who has to run for a psych eval every time he shoots somebody for good cause; that is you, son."

"Son? I'm not your son. I'm four years older than you."

"It's the way we talk in Kansas, where I am from. Everybody of the male persuasion is called either boy or son. Now stop parsin' me, less you like crossing guard duty at Wooster Middle School."

"At least I wouldn't have to shoot anybody," McGraw said.

"Don't bet on it," Carla said. "We caught lots of kids from that school packin' guns. You are a law enforcement officer in my department. You will either do your job the way I see fit, or you will take the train. You want a confab with some panty wearing psychologist? Fine with me. We got one, mandated by state law. Dude is a total asshole, like all the ones before him. Knock yourself out. But just remember; if he says you are not fit for duty, you are gone. Got it?"

"You'd fire me over something like that?"

"Like that," Carla said, snapping her fingers. "Better you go than gettin' your partner killed because you hesitated. Now go make a doctor's appointment. See Kennedy; he knows where the dummy's office is."

Office of Chief of Patrol Vito Antonelli

Stratford Police Department

900 Longbrook Ave.

November, 2008

"Yo, Barbie," Vito grinned when Carla came in. "Youse talk to that fanook McGraw?"

"I did."

"Youse help him?"

"I don't think so; he needs a different kind of help than I am qualified to give."

"I think he needs to get his ass kicked or shot before he'll wise up. Not killed, maybe just winged by a perp. I think he been pussyfied along the way. He married?"

"Didn't ask. That got nothing to do with how you do the job."

"He capped old Sammy," Vito grinned. "Half the force would like to put one in his ticker, but he always played the game. Took his pinch, pled out, and went back to doing his thing on the avenue. Never heard of him pulling a piece on anybody. That ain't Sammy's style. He was just an old nigger who dealt some shit."

Clarence Jackson walked by just as Vito said "old nigger."

"What you call me, Dago?" Clare exclaimed.

"Nothing, stupid. Nobody knew you was there; you take a bath or something? Usually you smell like fried chicken and wese can pick up on you a hundred feet away."

"Wese?" Clare grinned. "Fuckin' stupid Guinea bastard can't even talk English. What's this bullshit with McGraw? I just got back from a day off. He kill somebody? And what you grinnin' at, white bread?"

"Fuckin' big bubble butt, long armed tree swingin' watermelon pinchin' chicken thief," Carla said.

"Dumb ass cinder block head two bit tramp," Clare grinned. "Who McGraw shoot?"

"Your mama," Carla said. "Sammy Davis Junior."

"He already be dead."

"Sammy Williams Junior," Vito said. "Me and the douche bag was discussing pinning a medal on him."

"He killed that old brother? What for?"

"Says Sammy drew on him."

"Bullshit; Sammy don't pack a weapon. You got the piece, snowflake?"

"How the fuck should I know?" Carla exclaimed. "I got enough shit to do without McGraw's bullshit. He works for Vito, not me."

"How about it, Dago? Where's the gun?" Clare said.

"In your pants, Buckwheat. It just happened, already. Kennedy went to the scene and cleared the asshole. Gun must be in the evidence room."

Clare went to the evidence room and came back with the gun. He handed it to Carla. "Looky here; brand new Beretta 92F. Damn thing costs more than Sammy makes in a month peddling pot. Something ain't right here. No way Sammy could afford to buy one of these on the street. Check this out, honky."

"Fuck you," Carla grumbled. "I got shit to do."

"I got two words for you," Clare nodded. "Unemployment office."

"And I got two words for your ass; dead nigger."

"Remarks like that will not get you invited to dinner," Clare nodded.

"Good. I don't eat that greasy shit you jungle bunnies like."

"I know that old bastard; he don't try to kill cops. This don't look right."

"You think McGraw shot his ass and flaked him?" Carla said.

"Could be; the boy been complaining to people he been passed over. A good bust and a clean shoot might help him get a bump up."

"All right," Carla sighed. "I'll give this to Jackie Jasper. Vito, you put this asshole on school crossin' duty after he sees the shrink. That'll give us time to figure this out."

Stratford Police Department

900 Longbrook Ave.

November, 2008

"Hey," Jackie said as she walked up to Pat Kennedy's desk in the lobby.

"Hey what?" Pat said.

"Hey you."

Kennedy unwrapped a hot dog, leaned to one side, and ripped a terrible fart. "I have spoken," he smiled.

"Wrong language, toothless wonder," Jackie said as she backed up. "You should have been dead ten years ago, eating all those hot dogs."

"The Chinese hot sauce and jalapeno peppers keep my heart going," Pat said.

"Lucky us. You clear that McGraw shoot?"

"Indeed I did," Pat said. "One less drug dealer in Stratford."

"Chief Rastus says Sammy never packed, and would never shoot a cop."

"How times change," Pat said. "McGraw said he drew on him. We have the gun with Sammy's prints on it. That's a clean shoot in my book. End of story. What's the problem that has the diaper squad looking into this?"

"The prints are on the wrong part of the gun, genius. And there are prints on the ammo nobody ran. Not to mention it's a thousand dollar gun on the street, and it was reported stolen by a doctor who lives three houses away from McGraw. I'm going over to his office now. Maybe you should seek other employment; I hear Sabrett's is hiring. Bye."

"A pox upon thee!" Kennedy exclaimed. "Impugning my character like that. Stop at Duchess on the way back and get me six Planet Killers."

"Send one of your flunkies, Sergeant Garcia. I don't work for you."

"I'll forge your mommy's signature on your report card," Pat smirked.

"Eat hot dogs and die," Jackie sighed as she turned to go.

"Hey," Jackie said. "You Doc Hunley?"

"Yes," Hunley said as Jackie held up her badge. "Need something checked out?"

"What kind of doctor are you?" Jackie said suspiciously.

"Proctologist," Hunley grinned. "I'll give you a freebie. When is the last time anybody checked your colon?"

"My Uncle's birthday party two years ago. He loves his wheel chair," Jackie smiled.

"Oh, one of those tough girls, eh? I bet you work for Carla."

"I do. You know her?"

"You could say we're on intimate terms," Hunley smiled. "Nothing romantic, of course; that would be unethical. That doesn't mean I can't enjoy my work."

"I think more people than you have enjoyed working on Carla's keister," Jackie said. "You report a gun stolen?"

"Yes. Somebody broke into my home and took my Beretta. Did you find it?"

"Maybe," Jackie shrugged. "You have paperwork for the Mel Gibson Special?"

"Wasn't he great in those movies?" Hunley said as he rummaged through his desk. "I like the scene where he shot a smiley face at the range."

"Yeah, he's just ducky when he isn't getting shit faced and yelling shit about Jews." Hunley handed her the receipt, and she compared the serial numbers. "Yup, we got your gun," she said. "But you can't have it back just yet. It was used in the commission of a crime; it's evidence. You'll get it back when we're done with it."

"That could take a long time," Hunley said. "What do I do if I have to shoot somebody? Some of the girls who come in here don't like me poking around in their anal area."

"Gee, I wonder why not," Jackie sighed.

"How old are you, by the way?" Hunley said.

"Fifteen. You know, you remind me of the dudes Chris Hanson bags when they proposition young girls on the internet, then they show up at the girl's house in a raincoat, a Lone Ranger mask, and socks."

"I would never do a thing like that," Hunley huffed. "Do you go into chat rooms?" he grinned. "You're cute."

"You aren't," Jackie said. "Who investigated the break-in?"

"Some cop from Patrol. He poked around and said there wasn't any sign of forcible entry, and that I should just report the gun stolen and make an insurance claim."

"You get his name?"

"McGraw. Dale McGraw. Why?"

"Just wondering," Jackie shrugged. "We have to check every angle. Routine; just like when a hot teenager comes in here, you teach her how to apply the hemorrhoid cream with your finger."

"And they say being a doctor is boring," Hunley grinned. "I almost got caught one time; the girl realized I was applying the cream, but I had both hands on her shoulders. Took some fast talking to get out of that one."

"I bet," Jackie said. "Talk about no sign of forcible entry, huh? I bet you love poking around in some hot babe's ass."

"You have to be careful in my line of work," Hunley nodded. "I know what comes out of those things. I wear protective clothing and a face shield, and always follow the Proctologist's cardinal rule." He pointed at a sign on the wall next to his diplomas.

"Never squeeze their stomach," Jackie said as she read the sign. "Cute. Your mother make that for you?"

"How did you guess that?" Hunley grinned. "Sure you don't want that freebie?"

"Maybe another time," Jackie said. "My other Uncle's birthday party is coming up soon."

Wooster Middle School

Lincoln Ave.

November, 2008

"Hey," Jackie said as she walked up to McGraw with another patrolman. "How they hanging, Slick?"

"Well, this isn't the most exciting duty," McGraw said.

"You like action?" Jackie said.

"Not really. I had enough action this week. What's Miller doing here?"

"He's your replacement," Jackie said. "You're under arrest for the murder of Samuel Williams. Hands behind your back, and no funny stuff. I don't run very fast; you bolt on me, and I'll put one in your back."

"You can't be serious," McGraw said as Jackie cuffed him. "I was cleared on that shoot."

"You been uncleared," Jackie said as she pointed at the cruiser. "Get in the back."

"I want a lawyer and my union delegate."

"Can you at least wait until we get back to the fucking station?" Jackie said as her driver put the car in gear.

"Hey, McGraw," the driver grinned. "You're gonna look cute in a prom dress when they stick your ass in Osborn. What's your favorite color? I hear they sell matching shoes and accessories in the prison c"

"Shut up, Harrelson. That was a clean shoot. You have a lot of nerve arresting me, Jasper. What's your evidence?"

"Sorry, you lawyered up. We can't discuss your case."

"That's because you don't have one. Some department this is; I defend myself against a career drug dealer, and I'm the one who gets arrested."

"Life sucks, then you get twenty five to life," Jackie grinned. "Think of the benefits; you'll be able to yodel The Sound of Music out ot your asshole when you get out."

Stratford Police Department

900 Longbrook Ave.

November, 2008

"Siddown, stupid," Carla snarled at McGraw. "You too, Cantrell."

"That's Canfield."

"Whatever. Your asshole client is in a shit load of trouble."

"What did he do, steal your pizza?" Canfield said.

"Killed a drug dealer," Carla said. "And he lied to me. The second is worse than the first."

"Oh, I see…… the head of the terror squad is accusing a cop of murder. Gee, I never heard that one before."

"Fuck you, Cannoli. He's lucky I didn't grab him outside and dish out a little frontier justice."

"You have a thing for drug dealers all of a sudden? I hear you have a long row of notches on that Colt you pack, all courtesy of independent pharmaceutical entrepreneurs."

"Shit on you, and McGraw too. You and your big fuckin' words can kiss my Kansas ass. Boy is going up the lazy river by the old mill stream."

"Based on what? A clean shoot cleared by your own Sergeant?"

"I don't care who cleared it; he been de-cleared. Detective Jasper got the goods on his ass. Best you tell the boy to fess up; things will go easier on him."

"We intend to mount a vigorous defense," Canfield said. "He's innocent."

"You can mount your sister for all I care," Carla nodded. "He ain't innocent. We got the gun he stole from Doc Hunley, who just happens to live three houses away from him, and we got a nigger who will testify Sammy never drew down on Quick Draw here. He shot Sammy and planted that gun on him."

"Good luck proving that story," Canfield said. "See you in court. Come on, McGraw. Let's get out of here."

"He stays," Carla said. "He ain't been before a judge yet. You try to take him out of here and I will shoot the both of you."

"You on your period? You're awfully cranky today," Canfield said.

"Get out, Candido. This asshole stays in holding until he gets arraigned."

Bridgeport Superior Court

Golden Hill St.

Bridgeport, Connecticut

November, 2008

"State of Connecticut versus Dale McGuire," the bailiff intoned. "Murder, Robbery, Breaking and Entering, and Possession of a Stolen Firearm."

"Who represents the State?" Judge Allan Stevens said.

"District Attorney Brenda DiCenzo, Your Honor."

"And for the Defendant?"

"Attorney Rollins Canfield, Your Honor."

"How does your client plead, Mr. Canarsie?"

"Canarsie is in Brooklyn, Your Honor. My client pleads not guilty."

"Bail, anyone?" Stevens smiled.

"The Defense requests that the Defendant be released on his own recognizance."

"Brenda?"

"Is he like serious?" Brenda laughed. "The Defendant stands accused of murder; he is a police officer and is a flight risk. The People request remand."

"As Brenda pointed out," Canfield said, "the Defendant is a police officer. He has been on the force for some eight years and has a perfect record. He stands falsely accused of murdering a drug dealer, of which he was cleared by his Sergeant, and we will show that he acted in self defense."

"Bail is set at a million dollars, cash or bond," Stevens said.

"That's extreme, Your Honor," Canfield said.

"You asked for bail; you got it," Stevens said. "See the Clerk for a trial date. We are adjourned."

Bridgeport Superior Court

Golden Hill St.

Bridgeport, Connecticut

November, 2008

"Call Sergeant Pat Kennedy," Brenda said. Kennedy was sworn and sat down.

"What, no dress blues, Sergeant?" Stevens said.

"They don't make them in my size, Your Honor," Kennedy said. "I don't suppose I can eat hot dogs in court, can I?"

"No; only Beefaroni is allowed in my court room. Go ahead, Brenda; he's all yours."

"Sergeant Kennedy, did you receive a call to go to Stratford Avenue last week for a police involved shooting?"

"Yes."

"Who was the officer involved?"

"The Defendant Dale McGraw."

"Who did he shoot?"

"A drug dealer name of Samuel Williams, Junior."

"Did Mr. Williams survive?"

"No. He was pronounced dead at St. Vincent's Hospital."

"What did Officer McGraw tell you happened?"

"He said Williams pulled a gun on him, so he fired in self defense."

"Were you satisfied with his accounting of events?"

"He's a cop, not an accountant."

"Stop it, Kennedy!" Stevens laughed. "Only I am allowed to make jokes in court."

"It looked like a clean shoot," Kennedy shrugged. "The gun was by Sammy's hand."

"Did a Detective come to the scene?"

"No. I called Carla Larsen, but she was asleep. I didn't see any reason to have a big investigation."

"Was Mr. Williams well known to the Stratford Police Department?"

"Yes. He had a lengthy arrest record going back forty years."

"Was he ever arrested for possession of a firearm?"

"No."

"Was he ever arrested for assault or any other violent crime?"

"No."

"What was the nature of his arrests?"

"Low level drug dealing. He mostly sold marijuana in small quantities. Sometimes he sold Tylenol and other over the counter medications, claiming that they were amphetamines."

"But no weapons charges or violent crimes, correct?"

"Correct."

"Did you find it odd that a man with a non violent history would suddenly decide to shoot it out with the police?"

"After forty years on the job, I'm not surprised at anything I see. It did not fit his profile, but I've seen people change over the years."

"Nothing further."

"Sergeant Kennedy, you testified that Mr. Williams had always been a non violent person, correct?" Canfield said.

"Yes."

"How long has the Defendant been on the force?"

"Eight years."

"Had he ever patrolled Stratford Avenue prior to this incident?"

"Yes, many times. Every patrolman is assigned to every area of the town on a yearly basis."

"So would it be fair to say he knew Mr. Williams?"

"He may have," Kennedy shrugged. "I never asked."

"Do you recall Officer McGraw ever having arrested Mr. Williams?"

"Not that I recall, no. Sammy hadn't been arrested in several years."

"Can you think of any reason why Officer McGraw would want to murder a low level pot dealer?"

"No, I cannot."

"Has Officer McGraw ever been disciplined for violent behavior towards a suspect?"

"No."

"Nothing further."

"Redirect," Brenda said. "Sergeant, based upon the investigation that took place into this shooting, do you still conclude that it was a good shoot?"

"Objection," Canfield said. "That is for the jury to decide. Sergeant Kennedy's opinion might be prejudicial."

"Sustained," Stevens said.

"Call Detective Jacqueline Jasper," Brenda said. Jackie was sworn and sat down. "Detective, were you assigned to this case by Chief Carla Larsen?"

"Yes."

"Why did she think this incident needed investigating?"

"McGraw's report didn't match some of the evidence."

"Be more specific."

"The gun recovered was a nine millimeter Beretta 92F, a rather expensive pistol. One had recently been reported stolen by Dr. Jared Hunley, who lives three houses away from McGraw. The fingerprints recovered from the pistol were not where they should have been if Mr. Williams had fired the gun as claimed. That was probable cause to conduct an investigation."

"Did you interview Dr. Hunley?"

"Yeah," Jackie grinned. "That dude is weird."

"What did he say?"

"Well, he produced the sales receipt for the Beretta, and the serial number matches the weapon McGraw says he recovered from Sammy. He also offered to examine my … you know."

"No, we don't know," Brenda grinned. "Tell us."

"Bunghole," Jackie snorted. Stevens put his head in his hands.

"Objection," Canfield said.

"To what? Her bunghole?" Brenda grinned as Stevens convulsed in laughter.

"The relevance of her comments about Dr. Hunley being a … weird dude."

"But her bunghole is like okay?" Brenda said.

"Stop," Stevens gasped. "No more comments about bodily orifices, Detective. You too, Brenda. Get to something relevant."

"Did Dr. Hunley call the police when he found that his Beretta was missing?"

"Yes, he did."

"People's Exhibit 9," Brenda said. "Did he tell you verbally what had happened as to the missing Beretta?"

"He said he called the police," Jackie shrugged. "The responding officer was the Defendant. According to Hunley, the Defendant said he could find no signs of forcible entry and that Hunley should just file an insurance claim."

"Did you reinvestigate the break-in?"

"I did. I saw no signs of forcible entry either, and found no fingerprints other than Doctor Hunley's. I did find footprints in the dirt near the window, though. I took pictures and made a plaster cast for comparison."

"To what?" Brenda said.

"Police shoes."

"Was there a match?"

"Yes, as far as the type of shoe is concerned, but not to the Defendant's shoes, which he allowed me to inspect."

"What was the condition of the Defendant's shoes when you inspected them?"

"Brand new," Jackie said. "They even had that new leather smell."

"So he bought new ones and dumped the old ones, correct?"

"Objection, calls for speculation," Canfield said.

"Sustained."

"What size shoe does the Defendant wear?"

"Ten."

"And the plaster cast?"

"Same size; ten."

"Nothing further at this time."

"Detective," Canfield sighed. "Do you really think my client broke into Doctor Hunley's home?"

"Yes."

"Based on what?" Canfield laughed. "The nonexistent fingerprints?"

"Just a hunch. It's just too …. neat. Hunley's gun disappears, McGraw is the responding officer, next thing you know the gun winds up near a dead suspect's hand."

"But you can't prove the Defendant stole the gun, can you?"

"Not yet," Jackie said. "We're still working on that."

"Just like you're working on the Defendant's shoes, right? How many police officers on your force wear a size ten shoe?"

"I have no idea."

"Nothing further."

"Call Raymond Brown," Brenda said. Brown, an aging black man, was sworn and sat down. "Mr. Brown, please tell the jury where you live."

"1899 Stratford Avenue. Second floor."

"On the day Mr. Williams died, were you home?"

"I was home," Brown sighed. "I got no place else to be."

"Did you see the incident involving Mr. Williams and the Defendant?"

"I did," Brown said. "I saw it real good. I got perfect 20-20 vision, too. Don't need no glasses."

"People's 12, an independent eye exam conducted on the witness. He can see perfect," Brenda said. "Okay, Mr. Brown, did you know Sam Williams?"

"I did. I knowed Sammy for over thirty years."

"Did you know he sold marijuana?"

"Yeah," Brown shrugged. "Brother got to make a living. Everybody on the Avenue be into something crooked."

"Even you?" Brenda smiled.

"Yeah," Brown grinned. "I used to steal cars when I was young, and sell 'em to the chop shops. I ain't done that in ten years, though."

"To your knowledge, was Mr. Williams a violent man?"

"No, he was not. Old Sammy wouldn't hurt a fly."

"Tell the jury what you saw."

"Sammy were hangin' out in his usual spot near the hair salon. A cop car came up, stopped about twenty feet away, and he got out," Brown said, pointing at McGraw. "The Defendant."

"What did Sammy do?"

"Nothing; he just stood there. Cops don't usually hassle Sammy. The cop walked over to Sammy and they talked a bit. The cop frisked him and held up a small sandwich baggie with some stuff in it that looked like pot. Sammy said something back; I couldn't hear because it was cold out and the window was closed. They talked some more and then the cop looked around, then he pulled his piece and shot Sammy. When Sammy went down, the cop knelt down in front of him so's nobody could see, then he put a gun on the ground, close to Sammy's hand."

"What kind of gun did you see on the ground?"

"I know my guns; that was a Beretta like in them Lethal Weapon movies. I saw it real clear."

"And you are absolutely sure the Defendant had the Beretta, not Sammy?"

"I am. I saw the Defendant reach out and put the Beretta by Sammy's hand."

"Was Sammy known to be a man who carried a gun?"

"No. Sammy did not like guns. In thirty years, I never saw or heard of him having one. Besides, no old brother on the Avenue sellin' pot could afford one of them Berettas, even if he did want a gun."

"Your witness," Brenda smirked at Canfield.

"Mr. Brown, have you ever been arrested?"

"Yeah, a long time ago. Three times for car theft, no convictions."

"Did the District Attorney offer you anything in return for your testimony?"

"For what?" Brown laughed. "I got no warrants on me."

"But you are an admitted car thief," Canfield said.

"Ex car thief," Brown said. "I said I don't do that no more."

"So you say. What do you do for a living?"

"Handyman. You got anything needs fixing?"

"His case," Brenda muttered.

"What kind of gun do police officers carry in Stratford?"

"Glock nine millimeter is standard issue. You want to pack anything else you got to buy it."

"How far would you say you were from the Defendant when the incident occurred?"

"Right across the street, above him. About fifty feet."

"And you can identify different kinds of guns from that far away?"

"Yes."

"Let's find out." Canfield set up an easel at the opposite end of the court room and put a large piece of poster board on it. There were twelve different semi automatic pistols on the chart in three rows, life size. "There are twelve guns on that chart," Canfield said. "One of them is a Beretta 92F, and one of them is a Glock nine millimeter. Pick them out."

"Second one from the left, first row, is a Beretta 92F. Third one from the left, second row, is the Glock."

Canfield looked like he had just bitten into a shit sandwich. He took the easel down and went back to his table.

"Nothing further."

"Whoa, counselor; you didn't say if he got it right," Brenda said.

"Let the record reflect that the witness identified the correct guns," Canfield sighed.

"Conference, anyone?" Stevens smiled.

Canfield dutifully trudged into the conference room with his client, Brenda in tow.

"Is there an offer on the table?" Canfield said.

"Sure. What color jump suit does he want in prison?"

"Very funny. You have a weak circumstantial case at best. Try as you may, you cannot connect that Beretta to my client; all you have is the word of an admitted car thief."

"He identified your client and the gun. You got a witness that contradicts Brown?"

"I'm not going down there to interview those people," Canfield huffed. "I might not make it out of there alive."

"What a loss that would be," Brenda said. "My witness puts the gun in McGraw's hand. You got a witness that will testify he sold that Beretta to Sammy Williams? No, you do not. You got nothing, Canfield."

"I need more time. I have a couple of leads to check out."

"How much time?" Brenda said.

"A week."

"Okay," Brenda shrugged. "Let's go tell Stevens." They went back to the court room. "The Defendant wants a one week continuance to pursue new evidence. The People do not object as long as the Defendant stays locked up."

"Granted. The Defendant will remain a guest of the state. We are adjourned."

"A week corn-tinuance? What for? Boy is as guilty as hell," Carla said as she watched the Nemergut Brothers paint her new office.

"I don't know," Jackie said. "Canfield is up to something."

"Should have took that bastard McGraw for a ride to nowhere," Carla said. "One thing I do not like is a cop who kills people," she grinned. "Who the hell does he think he is, Judge Judy or somethin'?"

"Tell me you didn't say that," Jackie said. "Miss Home Depot."

"Ain't nothin' wrong with stake burnings," Carla said. "That is purification by fire. It is in the Bible."

"Oh; I guess that makes it all right then, huh?"

"Yes it does," Carla said. "Do not argue with the Almighty. Them boys all deserved what they got, and I gave it to 'em as only I can do. I even put barby-cue sauce on one of 'em, no charge."

One of the Nemergut Brothers turned around and stared at Carla. "Do you have to watch us paint?" he said.

"I kin watch you do anything I want long as you are in my po-lice station, you fuckin' crook. I ain't never seen you before. You a Nemergut?"

"Yes. My name is Jack."

"Last name should be Off," Carla muttered. "Don't be palaverin' with me; I ain't paying you to talk. Keep painting, and y'all better do a good job, too. And don't pull no shit with the bill, neither. I catch that snake Richie paddin' the prices, there will be hell to pay and one less Nemernuts in town."

"We would never do that," Jack smiled. "We're honest businessmen."

"Like that crook Dimitri at the Honeyspot," Carla said. "You know the Lovelace Triplets?" she grinned.

"No, but they sound divine," Jack said as he opened another can of paint.

"Do a good job paintin' my office and I will fix you up with them," Carla said. "They will drive you buggy, guaranteed. So, what y'all think Canfield be up to, Jackie?"

"He harped on not being able to connect the gun to McGraw. Brenda said so."

"Then let's pay the boy's house a visit and see if we can corn-nect it," Carla grinned. "He lives alone, and he is in the lockup. Me and Harper will do this."

"Without a warrant?"

"We will get one after we find out if there is anything in his house worthy of one."

"Wow, you should teach procedure at the Police Academy."

Residence of Dale McGraw

225 Nassau Road

Stratford, Connecticut

November, 2008

"Nice place," Harper whispered as Carla picked the lock on the front door. "How does he afford this on a Patrolman's salary?"

"That is what we are here to find out," Carla said. "Among other things." She pushed the door open and looked around.

"What are we looking for?" Harper yawned. "I need a nap."

"You ain't done shit in two weeks. No way you are tired."

"I had leadership courses to complete at the academy. Now that I'm next in line to be a Chief of Police after you drown in the bathtub some night drunk on your ass, I have to know what the job entails."

"Dogs got tails, not cops. Y'all was out banging Spanish dudes or somethin'; you are too damn stupid to pass no course at the academy. And you ain't getting' my job, neither. I do not bathe drunk."

"You don't bathe at all from the smell of things," Harper said, waving her hand in the air. "Is that your taco, or did you shit your pants?"

"Little of each," Carla grinned. "I been busy; I ain't had time to clean up. Check his desk; I am gonna check the refrigerator."

Ten minutes later, Carla was loading meat loaf TV Dinners into the microwave when Harper came into the kitchen. "Wait until you see this sick shit," she nodded. She tossed a file onto the table. "He's been running a human trafficking and murder for hire business with Applebaum."

"Applebaum?" Carla exclaimed. "That asshole couldn't find his ass with both hands. Boy been on the force nineteen years and is still a Patrolman Second Grade."

"Then he's faking it, or doesn't care if he moves up. He obviously doesn't need the money. He's probably using the job as cover."

"What the boys been doing?" Carla said, nodding at the file.

"They abduct kids for export to Saudia Arabia as sex slaves. Nine, ten years old, no older than twelve. When the Arabs are done with them, they send them back here to be swapped out, and Boy Wonder and his pal kill them. They also do paid hits for the Arabs."

Carla stared at the file for a long minute, then looked at Harper.

"Uh oh; I've seen that look before," Harper said.

"And you will see it again," Carla said. "Where does Applebaum live?"

"Stamford. Trump Parc, a 34-story condominium located at 1 Broad Street."

"We got to get McGraw released."

"Oh, sure; like Brenda won't see through that one."

"Okay, then let's arrange for the boy to escape from the North Avenue Jail."

"How?" Harper laughed.

"How the fuck should I know?" Carla exclaimed. "I just pay the bastards off. It's up to them to figure out how. Leave the fuckin' door open or somethin'. Always with the details; when you gonna learn? I will arrange it, then you meet me at Applefuck's place. That's where Quick Draw will go, guaranteed."

"Applefuck?" Harper giggled.

"Yeah. I am gonna bring somebody with me who has an interest in seein' them two suffer."

Residence of Don Applebaum

Trump Parc, 1 Broad Street

Stamford, Connecticut

November, 2008

"Hi, Donny," Carla said when Applebaum opened the door. "Can I come in? It's about a case I'm working on."

"I'm uh, kind of busy right now. Can it wait? How about tomorrow at the station?" Applebaum said.

"How about you open the fuckin' door before I fire your ass, Patrolman? I didn't drive all the way down here to listen to your bullshit."

"What's this about?" Applebaum said, maneuvering so that Carla couldn't see behind him.

"It's about this," Carla said, hitting the door with a vicious shoulder block. The door slammed into Applebaum's face; he reeled backwards and fell down. Harper came in, gun at the ready. She ran for the bedroom. A young girl came in and stood next to Carla.

"Come out come out wherever you are," Harper sang as she pushed the bedroom door open. "I know you're here, McMuffin. Don't make me waste perfectly good ammo on your worthless ass. Oh, and keep your paws where I can see them."

McGraw came out of a closet, his hands in the air.

"Oh, so you came out of the closet, huh? I always knew there was something weird about you. In the living room, Tutti Fruity."

McGraw went into the living room. Carla had put on gloves and had the window open, with Applebaum standing in front of it. "Over there," Carla said, motioning at McGraw with a silenced nine millimeter she had purloined from the evidence room. "Remember this girl?"

"No. Who is she? And what are you doing here?"

"Escapin' from prison is a capital offense," Carla grinned.

"Since when?" McGraw laughed.

"Since I am the one what caught your ass."

The girl walked over and stared at McGraw; he thought that it was like looking into the eyes of a demon. "You killed my sister," she whispered in a cold voice.

"Y'all be in the shit pile now, boy," Carla nodded. "This gal wants payback on your ass, and she means business."

"You get her away from me," McGraw squeaked. "You can't do this," he said.

"Yeah, you idiot," Applebaum said. "We're cops. You got a beef with us, you take us in."

"Who the fuck asked for your opinion, Applejack?" Carla said. She turned to Harper. "We need him?"

"Nope."

Carla shot Applebaum between the eyes; he rocketed backwards and fell out the window, plummeting thirty three stories into the parking lot. Carla tossed the gun after him.

"You killed Don!" McGraw exclaimed.

"You're smarter than you look," Carla said as she handed the girl a pair of surgical gloves and an evidence bag. "Too bad you fucked with the wrong people, huh smartass?"

The girl put on the gloves and opened the bag. She took out a switchblade knife while Carla spread a plastic tarp on the floor. She grinned at McGraw, who was starting to tremble and cry. "This is gonna hurt," Carla said. "A lot." She used duct tape to seal off McGraw's mouth. "No sense in botherin' the neighbors," she shrugged.

She went into the kitchen with Harper; the girl lunged at McGraw before he could react, and drove the knife into his groin. McGraw fell down onto the tarp in agony; the girl pounced on him and proceeded to cut him to pieces. She came into the kitchen a few minutes later, a weird smile on her face.

"All done," she said. "He's dead."

"And damn glad of it, I wager," Carla nodded. "Go clean up and change." She went into the living room with Harper; together they wrapped what was left of McGraw in the tarp and shoved him behind the sofa.

The shower started to run; the girl came back ten minutes later, her bloody clothes in a bag. She sat down at the table.

"This never happened," Carla said. "And you will never do anything like this again. You understand me?"

"Yes. Was what I did wrong?"

"No," Carla said. "Not in the eyes of God. But it was illegal, so you must never talk about this to anybody."

"Okay."

"Let's get out of here," Carla sighed. "I got work to do."

"Like what?" Harper said.

"Same shit, different day," Carla sighed. "And so it goes."

The End

Carla et all will return in ***Gone; Missing in America.***